Anna
the
Prophetess

Anna
the
Prophetess

a novel

Covenant Communications, Inc.

Published by Covenant Communications, Inc.
American Fork, Utah

Printed in the United States of America
First Printing: August 2018

22 21 20 19 18   10 9 8 7 6 5 4 3 2 1

ISBN 978-1-52440-679-0

Dedicated to Mindy Holt
a woman who, like Anna, is a great example of service

INTRODUCTION

The prophetess Anna lived during a remarkable era—that of the Messiah's birth and early years. Her name is the New Testament form of Hannah, and she is the only woman called a prophetess in the Gospels. Anna's family descended from the tribe of Asher, in which she was the daughter of Phanuel.

Unfortunately, Anna became a widow after a seven-year marriage, and there is no mention of whether she had children. She was, therefore, a woman whose life took a painful, unexpected turn. But as we will learn, Anna continued in her devotion to the Lord and determined to serve Him all the remainder of her days.

She is a testament to modern women that it's possible to live a life of joy even when struck with a severe trial. She carried an eternal perspective in her heart, and it's no small matter that she is heralded as a prophetess—one who draws close to the Lord and gains His utmost trust.

Interestingly enough, she never remarried but instead spent her remaining widowhood serving in the temple—a service time estimated at over sixty years. It's an impressive record of service in the public eye. Not many women are able to perform such an act away from home and for the public. She prioritized her time so she could be there, likely maintaining a residence near the holy place.

At the temple on Jesus's presentation day, we meet Anna as a woman "of a great age," of fourscore and four years (age eighty-four; Luke 2:37). With the completion of Mary's forty days of purification after giving birth, she and Joseph brought Jesus into Jerusalem. In Leviticus 12:2–5, we learn that for a male child, the woman was unclean for seven days and the additional days of purification lasted thirty-three days; for a female child, the woman was unclean fourteen days, and purification lasted sixty-six days.

Mary and Joseph were to present their newborn son to the Lord God at the temple, according to the law of Moses. Part of the presentation at the temple was offering a sacrifice of two turtledoves or two young pigeons in order to complete Mary's purification (see Luke 2:24). Simeon was the first to meet Mary and Joseph; he had been promised that he would not die before seeing the Messiah. He greeted the parents and took Jesus into his arms and prophesied regarding the salvation that had come to earth.

While Mary and Joseph "[marveled] at those things which were spoken" by Simeon (Luke 2:33), Anna entered the scene. Like Simeon, the Spirit led her to the Messiah and unmistakably informed her that this infant was the Redeemer.

Upon meeting the Messiah, Anna not only became a witness of the Messiah, but she also gave "thanks likewise unto the Lord, and [spoke] of him to all them that looked for redemption in Jerusalem" (v. 38). This notation leads us to believe that after Jesus and His parents fled to Egypt, Anna spoke reverentially about His birth and His presence on earth for as long as she lived. Her testimony may have been great before, as evidenced in her role as prophetess, but now it was magnified as she served as a sure witness to the Messiah's existence.

In this way, Anna's lifelong devotion to the Lord was no longer based on faith, but like the brother of Jared, she "had faith no longer, for [she] *knew*, nothing doubting" (Ether 3:19; emphasis added). What a wonderful gift! It is important for us to remember what preceded Anna's sure knowledge and what she embraced for at least sixty years of her life—it is something we cannot see or hear but only feel: faith.

Anna's devotion and role as a prophetess is further secured when we learn that she was the second woman in the Bible noted as fasting on a day other than the Day of Atonement (Esther was the first; see Esther 4:16). Fasting wasn't normally encouraged for women during ancient times, yet it seems that for Anna it was part of her spiritual regimen wherein she "served God with fastings and prayers night and day" (Luke 2:37). It was part of her journey toward becoming like her divine Father in Heaven, and it was this sort of devotion that led to the opportunity of meeting the infant Jesus and becoming a physical and spiritual witness to His mission on earth.

Anna's fasting was likely no easy task, especially at her age, but she recognized the importance of it in bringing her close to the Spirit, and as she continued to fast, her faith was strengthened. We do not know whether Anna recognized other signs of Jesus's birth that had been prophesied and taught for generations. There is no clear indication that anyone in the Old World knew of a prophecy in advance of the Savior's birth regarding a new star in the heavens, which would be a sign of His birth, but for this novel's purposes, sighting a new star is part of Anna's faith.

At the age of eighty-four, Anna became a true witness, and her unquestionable testimony has certainly blessed many lives. Her devotion to the Lord and her people, as well as the spirit of inspiration she cultivated in order to become one of the Lord's spokeswomen, marked her long life as a touching example of a divinely led woman. Like some of us, her life didn't turn out the way she had planned, yet she found ways to fill her life and devote it to the Lord. She moved forward with purpose and created a fulfilling life, giving us a wonderful example.

(Parts of the introduction were taken from the original publication of: *The Divinity of Women: Inspirations and Insights from Women of the Scriptures* by Heather B. Moore and S. Kent Brown, Covenant Communications, 2014.)

CHARACTER CHART

*Anna
Josiah, husband of Anna
Shoshana, cousin of Anna
Rachel, cousin of Anna
*Phanuel, father of Anna
Bethany, wife of Phanuel
Michael, son of Phanuel
David, friend of Michael
Benjamin, brother of Phanuel
Hannah, wife of Benjamin
Julia, great-niece to Anna
Silas, father of Julia
Eunice, mother of Julia
Philip, villager
Seth, brother of Philip
*Simeon, man at the temple
Tamar, Anna's neighbor in childhood village
Cyria, Anna's neighbor in Jerusalem
Matthew, Cyria's grandson

*Denotes historical figures

And there was one Anna, a prophetess, the daughter of Phanuel, of the tribe of Aser: she was of a great age, and had lived with an husband seven years from her virginity.

—Luke 2:36

CHAPTER ONE

Dry wind tugged at Anna's embroidered robe as she moved to the side of the road to allow a cart to pass. The spring gust had kicked up the dirt, and the passing line of carts heading to the temple made the dust bloom. An ancient donkey pulled the passing cart full of crates of doves, and a wiry boy who couldn't be more than fourteen or fifteen drove it.

Following in the wake of the dust cloud, a couple of shepherds urged a small flock of a dozen or so sheep forward. Lambing season had just ended, and the price of a lamb to be used as an altar sacrifice was at a premium.

Anna's heart tugged as she watched the procession. Another day of sacrificial offerings was about to begin, and the young animals would soon meet their death. The doves and the lambs would fulfill the laws and temple ordinances for those who had traveled to the temple from all parts of the Holy Land to make their offerings.

As the cart of doves and the fold of sheep gained distance on Anna, the road became quieter, and she enjoyed the early-morning repose before she joined with the bustle of temple work. The eastern sky was a riot of violet and pale gold as the sun pushed its way up, nearing the tips of the hills, ready to spill its rays across Jerusalem. Anna witnessed this display each morning as she left her home and never tired of the magnificence of the sunrise. Her steps were slow, and she gave herself plenty of time to make the journey. She'd lived a good many years on the earth, and she was grateful for each time she awakened to breathe in a new day. For it meant she had another chance to serve at the temple and dedicate her day to the Lord.

Most women who lived to her age were bent with physical ailments due to years of bearing children and raising them. Not Anna. Her husband had passed away decades ago, and there had been no fruit of their union. At least not in the form of children. Yet Anna did not regret her short marriage to her husband, and it was her life with him that shaped her life now.

The sound of another cart rumbling toward her brought Anna to the edge of the road again. With surprise, she recognized her neighbor's grandson, Matthew, who was no more than twelve. He was driving his grandmother's cart quite fast and recklessly, and the donkey being whipped into action looked as if he might rebel at any moment by tipping the cart and biting through his rope.

If Anna hadn't felt alarm shoot through her, she might have chuckled at the sight. She wondered what sort of errand Matthew was on so early in the morning and whether Cyria knew what type of driver he was. So, it was to her surprise when Matthew reined in the donkey as he neared where Anna stood on the side of the road. Had something happened to her neighbor and Matthew was coming to tell her?

"Whoa!" Matthew yelled, and the donkey came to a bumbling stop. The beast's eyes were drawn wide, and saliva edged its mouth.

"Matthew," Anna said immediately. "Is everything all right?"

"I think so." He wiped at his forehead with the edge of his tunic shirt. His dark, curly mop of hair was misted in dust from the road. "My grandmother sent me to fetch you."

Anna moved to the cart and gripped the edges, wondering if he was to deliver bad news after all. "Is she ill?"

Matthew frowned, then said, "Grandmother? No, she's not ill. She told me to bring you back home quickly because you have a visitor."

"A visitor?" Anna stepped back from the cart. "Surely everyone knows to visit in the afternoon. I've worked at the temple every morning for years."

"It's not a neighbor," Matthew said.

Anna tilted her head. Who else would visit her? She'd already paid her annual taxes, and she had no outstanding orders at the weavers.

Matthew scratched his head, then batted away a group of flies that seemed to like the scent of his skin. "Grandmother said the visitor is your nephew."

Anna stared at the boy. *Her nephew?* That could mean only one person. "Silas?"

Matthew shrugged. "I don't know his name."

"Was he with a woman and young girl?"

"There was a woman but not a young girl."

Anna's mind raced. Why would Silas and Eunice visit right in the middle of the olive-growing season? Silas owned orchards in her hometown, and if he was here with his wife, what did that mean? Had something happened to their child, Julia?

"I must go to them," Anna said, clutching her robe and turning to hurry down the road. Her pace was slower than she liked, but her body was only so nimble.

"Anna," Matthew called out. "I'm to drive you back. That's why I had to bring the cart."

Anna slowed and turned to see Matthew maneuvering the cart and stubborn donkey to now travel the other way. "Is it so urgent, then?" Anna asked, but Matthew didn't hear her over the donkey's rather loud complaints. "Heavens," Anna said as Matthew hopped down from the cart to extend his hand to help her inside. She preferred walking any day over riding in a bumpy cart, but by the determined look in Matthew's eyes, she knew she should concede. Besides, what were a few more aches and pains if she could reach Silas and Eunice quickly.

Matthew climbed back up into the cart, and they were off. Anna would have to get the donkey some fresh greens for all its trouble this morning, and all before the sun had fully crested the eastern hills.

As they traveled, Anna's stomach jolted with worry, exacerbated by the jarring movements of the cart, and she was grateful when they reached the road that turned off to her neighborhood. At last, they reached Cyria's home, but Matthew kept driving the short distance straight to Anna's.

Sure enough, a cart sat out front, one that must belong to Silas. She hadn't seen her nephew in many years, and she could only wonder at the reason for his visit now.

Matthew handed her down from the cart, and before he could make his escape, Anna said, "Thank you for fetching me, and thank your grandmother too."

Matthew nodded, and Anna turned toward the gate that led to the small courtyard of her home. There, standing in her courtyard, were two people. She recognized Silas right away. His beard was thick and full, and his hair was cropped short. He'd aged, but there was no doubt he was her nephew. The woman next to him, however, wasn't his wife, Eunice.

She looked to be about eighteen, and her long, plaited hair had come loose, as if she'd been awake all night. And perhaps she had because there were violet circles beneath her eyes. Then Anna realized she was looking at her great-niece Julia. She had grown into a young woman, no longer the child Anna remembered.

"Silas," Anna said. "Welcome. What brings you here? Is Eunice all right?"

"Eunice is as well as can be expected," Silas said, stepping forward and kissing Anna's cheek. He drew away rather brusquely, as if he had no time for greetings or pleasantries.

"Julia," Anna said, moving toward her. "You've grown into a lovely young woman." She was just about to embrace Julia when the young woman covered her face and turned away.

"Perhaps we should go inside and explain what is going on," Silas said, his tone firm. "We don't need to start the neighbors gossiping."

Anna looked from Julia to Silas. "Of course. Come this way. Have you broken your fast yet?"

"No," Silas said, following Anna inside the house, where she led the way to the cooking room. "We've traveled through the night."

Anna had so many questions, but it was clear that Silas was doing things his way. She stoked the embers in the hearth so she could warm water for a new batch of tea. Thankfully, she'd made honeyed cakes the day before and still had leftovers. She cut several slices and put them on the table in front of Silas and Julia.

Julia had sat across from her father, her hands in her lap and her gaze lowered. Occasionally, she sniffled, but otherwise, she remained quiet.

By the time Anna sat down and poured everyone a cup of tea, she was bursting with yet unanswered questions. She watched as Silas took a sip, then finally spoke.

"Anna, I must beg upon your hospitality," he said, looking into the steam rising from the cup. "Julia has refused a marriage proposal. As you know, the gossip is fierce, and the scandal will only grow—it is the way with small villages." He lifted his gaze. "We are in desperate need of your help."

Was it wrong for Anna to feel relieved? This was no report on Eunice's poor health or some other family tragedy. Yes, a broken betrothal was a very serious matter, but not the terrible event many made it out to be. Although it sounded like there hadn't been a betrothal yet. Anna lifted her chin. If there was one thing that years of working in the temple had taught her, it was to trust in the Lord in all things. Silas bringing Julia to her was no small matter of coincidence. Anna would do her best by her great-niece, come what may.

She placed her hand over Julia's, then met Silas's gaze. "Julia is welcome to stay with me as long as necessary."

CHAPTER TWO

JULIA PULLED THE BLANKET ABOUT her more tightly as the cool air of the spring night tried to make its way beneath. She could not sleep, and it was no wonder. This was her first night in her great-aunt's small home. Julia had been sent to live with Anna because the woman was growing more infirm in her old age. She was now fourscore and four years old. At least that was the story Julia's parents had given to the other villagers.

In truth, when Julia had refused to marry Bartholomew, her father had declared that if Julia wouldn't marry the man of her family's choice, she could learn what it was to live as a lonely, childless woman. Her father had brought her to Jerusalem, and everything about Julia's life had changed overnight.

Anna's small home was within walking distance of the temple of Jerusalem, to which she traveled each day to serve, preparing meals for the priests and keeping their robes in good repair. Julia hadn't seen Anna for years, so she didn't know her great-aunt well. She had heard that Anna had been a master seamstress in the days of her youth, and when she was widowed only seven years from her virginity, she had dedicated her life to the temple.

Julia admired her great-aunt's decision, but other villagers had thought Anna should have remarried. Since Anna and her husband had had no children, she had justified her actions by saying her womb was barren. And the Lord had led her to serve Him instead of remarrying.

In Julia's private thoughts, she viewed Anna as a courageous woman for not falling into the deep traditions of the village and marrying a widower to raise *his* children.

Julia, though, had no such excuse. She was nearly seventeen, past the time she should be betrothed. And although their community was small, situated on the west side of Jerusalem, there was more than one choice for a husband for Julia, but her parents had set their sights on only one man.

Bartholomew was older than Julia's own father's forty years, and his children were about Anna's age. She didn't want to marry a man who might make her a widow in a short time, leaving her a complex brood of children to watch over. How would she provide for them all? She knew that perhaps she was not the fairest woman to ever be born, but surely, one of the three other men in the village who were closer to her age and yet unmarried would be a more natural choice.

Most specifically, Philip.

But it was not to be. Julia had suggested Philip to her mother once and had been set down with a sharp retort that his mother's disgrace was too severe to overlook. Julia had heard the gossip five years before, when Philip's mother had abandoned her husband and children to join a traveling caravan. And it seemed that Julia's mother would not let such a taint be connected to *her* family.

Now, unable to sleep in an unfamiliar room, Julia sat up on her mat, tugging the edges of the blanket up to her chin. She was wide awake, restless, and felt as if her thoughts would never quiet. Something thudded on the other side of the wall near Julia's mat, and she flinched. "Anna?" she called out in a tentative voice.

No answer, but Julia then heard the shuffle of what sounded like footsteps. On high alert now, Julia rose from her mat, still clutching her blanket about her. Was there an intruder in the home? Or an animal?

Heart pounding, Julia moved to the doorway where a woven curtain separated the small room from the main part of the house.

Julia drew the curtain aside to see Anna's stooped form crossing the cooking room. The moonlight lay in patches about the floor, giving off just enough light to see that Anna held out one hand as if she were afraid of bumping into something, and gripped a mantle about her shoulders with her other hand.

Julia hated to startle her great-aunt, but she didn't know where the woman was going in the middle of the night. "Anna?" she whispered.

"Oh," Anna said, turning to peer in Julia's direction through the darkness. "I'm sorry if I awakened you." Before Julia could reply or question Anna, she continued, "The night is unusually bright. I want to take a look at the sky to see what's going on."

Julia blinked, not sure she understood her aunt. The woman was the oldest person she knew, so maybe she was speaking nonsense. Regardless, Anna shouldn't be going outside in the middle of the night.

"Wait." Julia crossed the room just as her great-aunt pulled open the front door.

It seemed that Anna wasn't interested in waiting. She walked into the small courtyard, and Julia followed. Her aunt then stopped and looked up at the night sky.

"Please come back inside," Julia said, touching Anna's arm. "I can make you some tea to help you sleep." Julia hoped she was saying the right things and offering the right comfort. She hadn't been prepared for a wandering elderly aunt.

Anna raised a hand as if she were telling Julia to be quiet. Her gray hair was loose from its usual long braid, gleaming silver in the moonlight as it tumbled over her thin shoulders. Even though she was a slight woman, she seemed to have a commanding presence about her.

Julia followed her aunt's gaze as she scanned the night sky. What was she looking for? What was she seeing that Julia wasn't?

"There," Anna said, pointing toward the east. "A new star. Do you see it?" Her voice was hushed, reverent somehow, and it sent a scattering of goose pimples along Julia's arms.

She'd never heard of a new star—but she wasn't a scholar. Her only talents included cooking and sewing. She didn't read or write—like Anna did—and Julia's sewing and cooking weren't unique enough to stand out from other women's in the village.

And Julia didn't know the maps of the heavens well enough to know whether a star had appeared or disappeared.

"It's the brightest one," Anna continued in a low voice. "Oh, my heavens." She stepped away from Julia and sank to her knees.

At first, Julia thought her aunt had fallen or perhaps fainted, but when Julia reached to grab her, Anna clasped her hands together as if she were offering a prayer.

"What is it?" Julia said, crouching next to her aunt. The woman had tears streaking her cheeks. Was she going mad? "Are you in pain?"

"It's the new star, foretold by the prophets," Anna said, her voice a trembling whisper. "The star is a sign of the Messiah's birth."

Julia stared at the brightest star she could see in the eastern sky. She'd heard the prophecies, of course, like any other Hebrew girl, but she couldn't say if the bright star in the sky was all that Anna claimed.

Anna leaned forward and placed her head on the ground.

Julia touched the woman's back, still wondering if she was all right. Anna's shoulders shook as if she were crying. But when she raised her head after several moments to look at Julia, she grasped Julia's hands and smiled.

"I did not know if I would live to see this day," Anna said in a reverent voice. "And now I can share it with you."

Julia suddenly found Anna's arms wrapped about her; she was surprised at her aunt's earnest affection. Her embrace was warm and comforting for someone Julia did not know well, but it was as if their shared heritage bound them together.

When Anna pulled away, she said, "Everything will change now; you will see." She ran a hand over Julia's cheek as if she were her dear daughter, a daughter she'd never had.

Julia looked over at the bright eastern star again. Out here, in the quiet of the courtyard, she could very well believe there was something special about the new star. But was this star truly the sign Anna was speaking about?

Julia settled by her great-aunt on the ground, and together they watched the night sky. Julia arranged part of her blanket over Anna to ward off the chill in the air.

"I have lived a good many years," Anna said, patting Julia's leg. "This, by far, was worth living so long without my husband. He would have loved to be here tonight, with me. Perhaps he is watching from his place in heaven."

Julia didn't want to discount anything her aunt was speaking about, so she simply listened.

"Someday, my dear," Anna continued, "you will find a man to marry and will raise a family."

Julia's throat tightened. After her father had left, they hadn't spoken of the reason Julia was in Jerusalem. Anna had told Julia to take a nap, which she had. Then, they'd prepared the evening meal together. Anna had spent the twilight hours working on an embroidery piece. Julia had cleaned up and spent a little time weeding the garden. There hadn't been much to do in the garden. Even in Anna's old age, she took good care of everything.

"You worry too much," Anna said when Julia didn't reply. "Do you not know that our Heavenly Father is in charge of everything? We just need to learn to bend to His will, which is always easier to say than to do."

Julia exhaled. "Is that how it was with you and your husband?" she ventured to ask. She'd heard a little about Anna's marriage, but since it had been a long time ago, anytime Julia asked about it, she didn't get very many answers.

"When I was a young woman, I had to have plenty of faith," Anna said. "For, you see, I lost my mother when I was ten years old.

I cared for my younger brother and father after that, so marriage was not something I hoped for in the way that many other young women hope for it. I had many responsibilities, but I loved feeling useful in caring for my father and brother. If I left, then what would become of them? Sure, my brother would eventually take a wife, but in the meantime, I needed to care for my father." She paused and exhaled. "I am grateful, though, that I didn't rush to meet everyone else's expectations. I let Heavenly Father guide me."

Julia thought about this for a moment. Had Heavenly Father guided her parents to select Bartholomew for her? It wasn't something she could very well ask them without sounding disrespectful.

"Did your father pick your husband for you?" Julia asked.

"Not at first," Anna said. "My husband picked *me*. It took my father—and me—awhile longer to come around."

This didn't bring Julia much comfort. She very well knew that this time spent with Anna was meant to bring Julia around to her parents' way of thinking.

"Have faith, my dear niece," Anna said, squeezing Julia's hand. "The Lord is mindful of you. Tonight a new star has been born, and we are witnesses to a miracle. If there's one thing I've learned in my lifetime, it is that you can put your whole trust in the Lord."

Julia exhaled and wished she could have as much assurance as Anna had about life's challenges and choices.

CHAPTER THREE

When Julia awoke next, light flooded through the small window in her chamber, telling her she'd overslept. She should be up and helping Anna. Then Julia remembered . . . the new star in the heavens they'd seen the night before, the hours they'd spent talking once they'd returned to the house, and how Anna had told Julia to sleep in as long as she needed this morning.

Julia looked about the small but tidy room. She couldn't hear any sounds from within the house, so she wasn't sure if Anna was awake or not. Listening carefully, Julia made out the pounding of children running or playing in the road outside. Then she heard the chatter of a group of birds most likely perched in the pomegranate tree in the back courtyard.

She fought back a yawn as she rose from her mat and folded her blanket. Day two of her exile had arrived. The sound of humming reached Julia, and she knew that noise came from outside. She crossed to the window and peered out at Anna in the garden, who was harvesting a few cucumbers. The woman must have returned from the temple already and hadn't even paused to rest.

Yet Julia had never been around someone who was so content with life and her own self as Anna seemed to be.

Julia pulled on her outer robe and joined Anna outside at the edge of the garden plot.

"Ah, there you are," Anna said when she saw Julia. "How did you sleep?"

"Quite well." Julia squinted up at the sky to gauge the position of the sun. It was nearly midday by her estimate. She focused back on Anna. In the light, her hair was a pale gray. She wore a dark green tunic that matched the deep color of her eyes. Wrinkles lined her face, but she was still beautiful. Even at her age, she still moved with elegance as she worked in the garden.

For a moment, Julia imagined Anna as a young woman—with the cherished beauty of youth and a heart full of hope. By looking at Anna now, one wouldn't know she'd lived a life of barrenness and had been married only a short time. Yet Anna had found a way to live a fulfilled life.

"Did you sleep?" Julia asked Anna.

The woman smiled, pushing up the wrinkles on her face. "At my age, sleeping is more like napping. I haven't had a full night's sleep for many years. But I look at the quiet, wakeful moments during the night as tender mercies from the Lord. I do my best thinking then, and I can reflect upon my blessings without distractions."

Julia didn't know whether to be awed or to laugh at her aunt, who had the strangest perspectives about the difficulties of life.

"What can I do to help you?" Julia motioned to the basket of cucumbers Anna carried. "You can sit in the shade while I finish the garden work. Just tell me what else you'd like harvested."

"Oh, I am finished," Anna said, lifting the basket.

For such an aged woman, Anna was still sturdy, Julia decided.

"I'm taking these to my neighbor," Anna said. "Her garden was attacked by insects last week, and much of her produce was destroyed. Come with me. I'd like you to meet my neighbor Cyria."

"All right," Julia conceded. "Let me carry the basket for you though."

Anna gazed at Julia as if she were about to contradict her. Instead, she said, "Thank you for your help. It's a blessing to have you in my home."

Julia's heart warmed at the kind words. She'd felt anything but appreciated over the last few months back home.

The women walked around the house and out the front gate. A group of young children was playing a game with a long stick and a rock. Their laughter made Julia smile. One of the young boys turned to watch them pass, then waved at Anna.

"They're dear children," Anna said. "And always friendly to me." Her tone sounded wistful, and Julia wondered if Anna wished she had children of her own.

"This is Cyria's home," Anna said, slowing in front of a well-kept homestead.

The house was about three times larger than Anna's, and the courtyard was paved with smooth stones. An elegant fountain, its base inlaid with colorful mosaic tiles, rose in the center of the courtyard. They crossed the courtyard and knocked on the front door. A girl of maybe ten or eleven opened the door. Her dark eyes brightened when she saw Anna.

"You've come," the young girl said. "My grandmother will be so pleased."

"Wonderful." Anna smiled. "I've brought my great-niece Julia to visit as well."

"Is that Anna?" a woman's voice called from inside the home.

Anna stepped inside, and Julia followed. A woman came toward them. She was perhaps in her sixtieth year, and she wore a lavender tunic embroidered with delicate stitching. The woman's dark hair was streaked with gray, but it only made her look lovelier. "Hello, I'm Cyria," she said to Julia.

"I'd like you to meet my great-niece Julia," Anna said.

"Welcome to my home," Cyria said, then she looked at Anna. "I was hoping you'd come." Cyria kissed Anna's cheek in greeting.

"We've brought cucumbers." Anna motioned to the basket that Julia carried.

"Oh, you didn't have to bring a thing," Cyria said, taking the basket Julia offered. "You are always doing something nice for me."

Julia watched the women's interchange with interest. It was plain that Cyria enjoyed many more luxuries than Anna—yet Anna was bringing produce from *her* garden. The front entryway of Cyria's home opened into a large, elegant room. Vases and artwork decorated the room, and soft piles of cushions rested atop a thick rug.

"Come with me to the market this morning," Cyria said. "We'll look at the trinkets from the traveling merchants."

"You know I don't want anything fancy," Anna protested.

"I know, but what if you can find embroidery thread or a length of woven cloth to use for the temple?" Cyria asked. "Let me buy something for you to repay all of your kindness."

"I don't need repayment," Anna said.

"Then let me thank you for being such a good friend." Cyria seemed to be winning the argument because Anna smiled. Cyria turned to Julia. "Will you accompany us as well?"

Julia had been to the main Jerusalem market only a few times when she was much younger. Her mother preferred to shop in their own village, and her father didn't want Julia exposed to such worldly travelers and merchants. She could not turn down such an offer. Besides, she'd be completely safe traveling with two widows. "I suppose I could come along."

Both women smiled at her. "You'll love it," Cyria said, linking her arm with Julia's. "First, let's have tea and honey cakes. Then we'll set out on our journey."

An hour later, Julia sat next to Anna in a cart that Cyria had asked one of her servants to prepare. A man of about thirty drove the cart, and they bumped down the road, past small homes similar to Anna's, as well as larger homesteads. They even passed a few estates that made Julia curious as to what type of lives the residents led behind their high walls.

Julia listened as Anna told Cyria about the new star from the night before.

"You'll see it again tonight in the eastern sky," Anna said.

"We shall look at it together, then," Cyria said. "Which means you should stay for supper. We don't want those cucumbers to go to waste."

As they neared the market, the road grew more congested with other carts, donkeys loaded with bundles, and even a few camels being led by their masters. Julia's anticipation increased.

The final bend brought them in view of the dozens of merchant carts and open-sided tents surrounding the large square, as well as makeshift pens that corralled animals for sale or trade. There were hundreds of people, and the sheer number of so many people in the same place was exhilarating to Julia.

"We should visit the spice merchants," Anna said. "Julia's father told me she's a wonderful cook."

Julia wasn't sure if that was exactly how her father had described her cooking skills, but she did very much want to look at the spices. What would it be like to try out spices she'd never tasted before?

As the older women climbed off the cart first, Julia took the time to look about the market from her high perch. The scent of baking bread teased her senses, and she spotted a group of Bedouins camped beneath a copse of trees, making their own supper. One merchant displayed a variety of statues no larger than the palm of her hand. They were statues of different gods and goddesses, primarily Baal.

Another merchant was selling beads and other trinkets. Several women clustered around the cart, engaged in a fierce, verbal bargaining exchange. On the other side of a cart selling sheep's wool sat a makeshift shelter providing shade to a couple of coppersmiths and silversmiths who were pounding and shaping tools for waiting customers.

Julia turned away from the sight of the coppersmith hut. It reminded her too much of Philip. He and his brothers were the village blacksmiths, and just the sight of this shop brought the image of Philip to mind. She knew she missed him, but until this moment, she hadn't realized how much.

Would it always be this way? Every time she heard the sound of a blacksmith's hammer, would she think of Philip?

Anna linked arms with Julia as they walked through the market, and Cyria linked arms at her other side. They took their time, investigating many of the merchant carts, yet buying nothing. When they reached a cart full of finely woven fabric, Anna's eyes brightened.

Julia almost laughed at her great-aunt's enthusiasm as she examined every length of fabric and looked through the spools of thread as if they were made of precious silver. Despite Anna's protests, Cyria bought her three spools of thread and a length of woven fabric.

When they reached one of the spice merchants, Julia's senses were assailed with the variety of scents. The merchant, a short, rotund man, was more than happy to explain the different spices and their flavorings.

Anna and Cyria waited in the shade of a nearby lean-to to give Julia all the time she needed to examine each basket and barrel.

"Julia?" someone said behind her. A man's voice.

She turned yet couldn't quite comprehend what she was seeing. A tall man stood before her, his shoulders broad and his dark hair tied back from his perspiring forehead. She'd know his brown eyes anywhere. "Philip?" she said. "What—? How did you . . . ?"

He grinned in that easy way of his, in the way that had stolen her heart.

"My brother Seth and I are taking my father's place at the market this month."

Then Julia remembered. Philip's father came to the Jerusalem market during the harvest seasons since so many more traveling merchants visited and the demand for blacksmithing work increased beyond what the Jerusalem blacksmiths could handle.

It was probably why Julia hadn't seen Philip for the past two weeks. She wondered if he even knew about her exile.

"I wasn't expecting to see you here," Philip said. "Well, honestly, I would expect to see you looking at a spice merchant's cart."

A thrill ran through her at the observation.

"Are you here with your family?" he continued.

"No. I mean, yes," Julia said. She couldn't get over the fact that of all the places her father could have sent her to forget about any aspirations to marry Philip, she was standing in front of the very man now. "I'm staying with my great-aunt Anna just west of here."

"Oh, the temple worker?" Philip said, his expression relaxing as if it were good news that she wasn't with her family—more specifically her father.

Although Philip hadn't ever formally spoken to her father about marriage, she knew enough from his younger sister that Philip had discussed her with his own family.

"I haven't heard anything about you coming here," Philip said. "How long will you be staying with your great-aunt?"

Julia had a hard time focusing on what Philip was saying because she was suddenly feeling miserable. How could she marry Bartholomew and see Philip about the village while he was married to another woman? Would she always feel this way when she saw him? A mixture of exhilaration and misery?

She had to tell him. Now might be her only chance to explain things. She glanced to where Anna and Cyria were looking at a row of painted vases.

"I need to tell you something, Philip," Julia said, moving a step closer and lowering her voice.

He looked down at her as if surprised at her boldness for standing so close, but she didn't want to be overheard by anyone else.

"My parents want me to marry Bartholomew." She noted the darkening of Philip's eyes, but she had to say this all at once or she would lose her courage. "I refused, and so my parents sent me to live with Anna. They want me to witness what it would be like to live a lonely life without a husband and children." Tears burned her eyes, and she cursed the moisture, but it would not retreat.

Philip studied her with those brown eyes of his. "Why did you refuse Bartholomew?"

Did Philip think her a fool for doing so? She knew she had to confess all, even if they were standing in the middle of a crowded marketplace. She lowered her eyes, although she could still feel his gaze on her. "I refused to marry Bartholomew . . . because someone else has my heart." She couldn't look at him. She didn't dare.

A moment passed, then two as the sounds of conversation, laughter, and merchants calling out their wares faded around them. It was like Julia and Philip were in their own quiet cocoon, a cocoon that held her most precious secret.

Philip took her hand for a brief moment, and his thumb brushed over her fingers. Julia thought her heart might stop. He released her hand quickly, then he leaned slightly closer, his own voice low. "Our village isn't the only place we could live."

Julia's gaze snapped to his. He wasn't smiling but was watching her intently. "What are you saying?" she whispered.

"We could live somewhere else," Philip said. "But you have to understand what you'd be giving up, and if it would be worth it."

She exhaled. Did he think she was a fool? Or was he saying it was all right that she not marry Bartholomew? Or was Philip asking her to take a chance with him? Defy her parents? A breeze kicked up, and she lifted a hand to smooth back the strands of hair that had escaped her braid, but Philip was faster. His touch was light, barely there, yet it burned all the way to her heart.

He lowered his hand all too soon. "Julia, I can work in any town or village with my trade, but you must understand that if your parents disown you, there would be no going back. Our children would never know your parents."

Tears burned in her eyes again, and she blinked them back, wishing she were a stronger person. Wishing Philip didn't have to see her cry.

"What about you?" she asked, her voice cracking. "What do you want?"

"You, Julia. It's always been you," he said without a single moment's hesitation.

CHAPTER
FOUR

JULIA COULD ONLY STARE AT Philip as he spoke. Had he really told her that he was interested in her . . . to be his *wife*? He hadn't said it in so many words, yet she had no doubt as to what he meant.

She felt warm to her very toes when he said, "We wouldn't be the first couple to marry without a parent's consent."

And that was what it would be, she knew. Philip was right. If they married, she would be cut off from her family. Her parents might even be shamed by other family members and neighbors. Her actions would affect not only her and her family, but they would affect Philip's family too.

"What about you . . . and *your* family?" she asked.

Philip was still standing close to her, and his fingers brushed her hand for the barest of moments. "We will create a new family."

Tears filled Julia's eyes again. She had not expected such declarations from Philip—here or ever. She had let her hope fade, and now, it was starting to bloom once again.

"Who is this?" someone said, coming up to them.

Cyria and Anna had arrived, and both women looked at Philip expectantly. He bowed his head and said, "I'm Philip, son of Aaron, from Julia's village."

Julia was grateful she hadn't told Anna the name of the man she'd hoped to marry, or this meeting would be very awkward. But Anna's gaze appraised Philip, and Julia knew that somehow Anna had drawn her own conclusions.

As Philip pointed over to his blacksmith tent and explained what he was doing at the market, Julia tried to calm her racing heart by taking a few deep breaths. Had she and Philip really had a conversation about marriage? When he looked back at her, his smile was warm, his eyes searching.

Julia allowed herself to smile back. Perhaps Anna was right. Perhaps Julia should have more faith. How had Philip happened to see her in such a large and crowded market? And how had she had such courage to say the things she had? And here he was, speaking with all three of them and clearly winning their regard.

Julia realized she hadn't been paying attention to the conversation until she heard Cyria say, "You and your brother must join us for supper this evening."

Julia hadn't expected such an invitation. She looked at Anna in surprise, but her great-aunt merely gave her a knowing smile. Philip readily agreed, sending her a glance of triumph. This only made her blush and then start to feel nervous. If her father found out, what would he do?

When Philip bade everyone goodbye and returned to his blacksmith tent, both Anna and Cyria turned to look at Julia.

"He is a fine man," Cyria said. "And he is very interested in you."

Julia's face heated. "I—"

Anna linked her arm with Julia's. "We understand, dear. We were young once. Come, finish picking out your spices, then we'll return home. We've guests to prepare for."

Cyria laughed. "That we do. Is Philip's brother as handsome as he is?"

Julia was surprised at the question. "They have similar features," she admitted. "Seth is married with a young family."

"And Philip?" Cyria prompted.

"He is yet unmarried," Julia said.

She turned from the women then, unwilling to let them see her blush. She busied herself by asking the spice merchant the prices of his various goods. Once she'd picked out a few of them and Anna had made the purchase, the women walked back to the cart that would take them home. Julia looked toward the blacksmith tent a final time, but the crowd prevented her from seeing Philip or his brother.

On the journey back to Cyria's home, Julia found that her thoughts were disjointed. She worried that somehow her father would discover she'd be spending time with Philip and his brother tonight. Would that create conflict between her father and Anna for allowing the shared meal?

Once they reached Cyria's home, Julia and her aunt excused themselves for the time being to return to Anna's home. Julia insisted on carrying the thread and cloth that Cyria had purchased for Anna.

The two women walked in silence the short distance to Anna's house. Once inside, Julia helped Anna organize her purchases, then set out the spices she'd picked out. She'd told Cyria she'd bring a dish for the supper.

Anna sat on a stool and began to work on some embroidery while Julia created a meat sauce with her new spices.

"Is Philip the man you have fallen in love with?" Anna said.

The question was so direct that it seemed to jolt right through her. Julia searched for an answer she could give her aunt. "He has been a friend since childhood, and we get along quite well."

"Do your parents know about your affection for him?" Anna pressed.

"I brought his name up to my mother once, but she immediately discouraged the idea of any connection between our families." Julia had no doubt that her mother had shared this with her father. "Philip's mother abandoned her family to join a traveling caravan."

"Ah," Anna said. "I can understand their concern. Small villages can be unforgiving sometimes. Have no fear. The Lord knows your heart, and He wants you to be happy."

Julia stared at her aunt. How could Anna continually give such assurances? It was hard to comprehend always having so strong a faith. Julia lowered her gaze, feeling new tears start.

Anna rested her hand on Julia's arm. "What is it, dear?"

"My father will never allow me to marry Philip because of the stain on his family," she said. "If I don't consent to marry Bartholomew, my parents say I will be alone and miserable the rest of my life." She didn't realize how her words sounded until it was too late. She met Anna's steady gaze. "I'm sorry. I didn't mean to insult you."

Anna's smile was soft. "I am not offended. I know your parents' intentions are worthy, and I know what many people thought when I chose never to remarry. It's a long story and one I have rarely told. Perhaps someday I'll tell you."

Julia felt goose pimples rise on her skin. "I'd love to hear your story." No one in the village had been able to come up with a reason why Anna would refuse to marry a second time and instead devote her life to serving in the temple.

"Perhaps you'll be the one I tell it to," Anna said.

When Julia finished making the meat sauce, they walked over to Cyria's home. The sun had sunk below the horizon, but the sky was splashed with orange and gold, so they had plenty of light. As they crossed the front courtyard and neared the door, Julia heard the deep rumble of male voices coming from within. It seemed that Philip and Seth were already here.

Cyria's granddaughter opened the door again and ushered them inside to where several people were standing in the front room, including Cyria's son, his wife, and other children.

"Welcome, welcome," Cyria said, stepping forward and kissing Julia's cheek, then Anna's.

Julia didn't meet Philip's gaze directly, although she knew he was looking at her. She still wore the same clothing she'd worn to the market but had re-plaited her hair and put on her gold earrings she'd received for her birthday last year. Cyria made introductions and then directed everyone through the hallway that led to the rear entrance of the house.

The back courtyard was lit with torchlights, and a long, low table was surrounded by piles of cushions for the guests to recline and sit on.

Philip was seated across from Julia so that every time she looked up, she saw him. She remained quiet for the most part as Cyria and her son asked Philip and Seth about their lives and blacksmithing. Seth answered questions about his wife and children, and at this point, Julia felt Philip's gaze on her. She looked at him and wished they weren't always surrounded by people. His words had made her think about what she wanted her future to look like. She couldn't imagine a life permanently away from her family, but what about a life without Philip?

The lump in her throat tightened as she thought about the unfairness of having to choose. Why couldn't her parents overlook Philip's family situation? Surely, he was not responsible for his mother's failings. His brown eyes stayed focused on her as the conversation floated around them.

Julia's heart drummed beneath the intensity of his gaze, and it was like she knew he too was thinking about their conversation at the market. He was asking her if she was willing to make such a sacrifice.

She exhaled and looked down at her food. She'd been moving it around her plate for most of the meal and had hardly touched it. Was she ready to follow her heart? Did she have the courage? She looked back at Philip, and their gazes connected immediately. She wanted to nod, but she felt like this was bigger than just her decision alone. She needed to talk to someone—perhaps Anna—even though she knew what Anna's answer would be. Ask the Lord.

Julia sent Philip a tentative smile. She had a plan of action now, and she was determined to follow it. When Philip smiled back, Julia hoped that whatever the Lord told her to do, she'd have the courage to do it.

When the meal was finished and cleared, the servants brought tea, and the guests lingered to talk. As the hour grew late, everyone rose, and the group walked around the house to the front courtyard, where the moonlight was their only guide. Cyria kissed each of the men's cheeks and told them it was wonderful to get to know them. Anna did the same, and when it was Julia's turn to bid her farewells, she clasped Seth's hand.

"Take care of yourself, Julia," he said with a smile that was so much like his brother's. He released her hand, then moved toward the gate to leave.

Then Philip moved to stand in front of her, and when he grasped her hand—much like his brother had—Julia felt the difference in his touch. The warmth of his skin seemed to travel up her entire arm.

"Will you be at the market tomorrow?" Philip asked in a low voice. "I'd like to speak with you privately."

"I will try." Julia glanced over at her aunt. She didn't know how she'd arrange everything. "I'm not sure if my aunt will allow it, so I might have to try to slip away. How long are you in Jerusalem?"

"We'll be here for a few weeks," Philip said. "Until the crowds die down."

Julia nodded, and Philip squeezed her hand and let go. The loss of his touch made her forlorn but also more determined. She stood with the women as the men went out the gate, waved a final time, then set off toward wherever they were sleeping for the night.

"Walk out to the road with us," Anna told Cyria. "The new star from the east still burns bright."

Anna linked arms with Julia, and Cyria walked beside them. The road was dark and quiet, but the air seemed to thrum with life beneath the glowing heavens.

"It really is beautiful," Cyria said in a quiet voice as they stood together, looking up.

"Whenever I watch the heavens at night, it brings me a sense of peace," Anna said.

Cyria looked over at Anna. "That it does."

The women watched the star for a few more moments, each lost in their own thoughts, with Julia wishing she could feel the measure of peace that Anna felt. Eventually, Cyria bade them farewell and returned to her home.

Julia and Anna began the walk back to her home.

Julia gazed at the star as they walked, wondering if she'd ever have the answers she was seeking. Finally, she looked over at Anna. "How can you feel so much peace all of the time? It seems you have the same answer for every problem that arises."

"You are troubled," Anna said without preamble.

Julia took a deep breath. "I am." She hoped she could trust her aunt with what she needed to say. "I've an important decision to make."

They were nearly to the house, and Anna said, "Come inside, then. Let's make some tea. I sense that we both have stories to tell tonight."

Moments later, they sat in the cooking room, with an oil lamp on the table and two cups of tea between them.

Julia sipped the tea, then took a deep breath. "Earlier at the market, Philip made his intentions plain. He told me that if my parents didn't approve of our match, we could find another place to live."

Anna didn't speak right away, and she took a sip of her tea. "You have many options before it comes to that."

Julia nodded. She'd expected this from her aunt, even though she'd been living with her for only two days.

"Tomorrow, I'd like you to come with me to the temple," Anna continued. "You will be witness to many things that will give you a broader perspective of life. I also want you to meet Simeon. Years ago, he had a revelation that he would not die until he had seen the promised Messiah."

Julia hadn't argued about the sign of the new star, but this new claim about Simeon was something she hadn't heard before. "How old is Simeon?"

Anna's face crinkled into a smile. "Older than I."

"And . . . do you believe he will truly live to see the Messiah?"

Anna's smile remained as she said, "Don't forget the star in the east."

How could she? Her aunt had spoken about it many times. Yet, despite Julia's skepticism, something about her aunt's confidence sent peace through Julia.

"I would love to meet him," Julia said and found that her answer was honest. She needed to feel peace since desperation over Philip was setting in. It would take a miracle to get her father to allow her to marry Philip.

As usual, Anna didn't miss anything, and she seemed to guess every one of Julia's thoughts. "If you'd like, I will speak with your parents about Philip," Anna said.

Julia was grateful for the offer. But she worried that if Anna spoke up, her father would know all that had transpired to get to this point. He would not be pleased with any of it. Her father would regard her meeting Philip in the market and eating supper with him at Cyria's home as serious offenses.

"I don't want my father's anger turned toward you," Julia said. "You have made me feel so welcome here and have been so patient with me. I don't want you to be hurt by my stubbornness."

Anna gave a soft chuckle. "Know that I have reached an age where I cannot be hurt by another's stubbornness. I don't know how many days I have left upon this earth, and I rejoice that I have lived this long, but I cannot let you suffer in silence. If I can be your voice on this occasion, it would be a great honor."

"I will think about it," Julia said. It was the best reply she could give.

"All right, I will agree to that. And tonight, we will pray for the Lord's help." Anna patted Julia's hand. "You will see and learn much tomorrow at the temple, but most importantly, you must learn to listen and learn with your full heart. Soon, all of Jerusalem will understand the significance of the new star in the east."

Julia wasn't entirely clear on what her aunt meant, but she was definitely curious. "I'm looking forward to visiting the temple with you." Her aunt nodded and seemed to be in a perfectly mellow and talkative mood. Perhaps now was a good time to see if Anna would talk about her early years.

"Will you tell me about your husband, Josiah?" Julia asked, hoping she wasn't overstepping any boundaries.

"Ah," Anna said, a faint smile lifting her lips. "Perhaps it would be good for you to hear about my beloved Josiah. Some days, it's as if I just bade him farewell in the morning before he goes to teach his students. Other days, I wonder if I can continue waiting to see him again."

"Was he much older than you?" Julia prompted, hoping that her aunt would tell the whole story and not cut anything out.

Anna's gaze was steady on Julia when she said, "Josiah was only a few years older than I. He was widowed, you know. His first wife died in childbirth. He moved to our village shortly after his loss— to escape all the memories, I suppose, and to begin anew." She shook her head as if she sympathized. "Life is difficult for everyone, but we can find happiness if we're diligent. We all need to ask the Lord what His will is for us. When I first met Josiah, I didn't think I'd ever seen such sadness in a man's eyes. I suppose my heart went out to him then and there. I had lost my own mother at a young age, and I had seen the heartache my father had endured. With Josiah, though, it would be some time before I let myself admit my feelings for him."

She paused to take another sip of her tea, then she continued. "Life does not turn out as we plan, my dear. But if we keep our faith and rely on the Lord, we will begin to understand the purpose of our challenges."

"How old were *you* when you met Josiah?" Julia asked.

Another smile crossed Anna's face. "I'll start at the beginning."

CHAPTER
FIVE

67 Years Before the Birth of the Messiah

"ANNA, THE MEN ARE WALKING home from their lessons," Shoshana said.

Anna looked up from her embroidery to see that her cousin Shoshana had put down her own stitching and was looking out the front widow. "It is that time of day," Anna said in a dry voice.

The men gathered on select afternoons to study the Mosaic law and learn from the scribes of the village—an occupation in which her father served. He was one of the head scribes and taught the Mosaic law at the synagogue to the boys and men of the village.

"If only one of them would seek my hand in marriage," Shoshana continued. She was seventeen, six months older than Anna, and frequently bemoaned the fact that she was not yet betrothed. Most women in their village were betrothed by fifteen, if not already married, but it wasn't exactly a terrible fate to wait a year or two for the big event. Shoshana was curvy for her age, and her long dark hair fell in waves down her back. She would not be overlooked for long.

"You'll be wed and expecting a child before you know it," Anna replied. For herself, she could wait. She was seventeen now but was in no hurry.

Their home was only a short walk from the synagogue, so all the male students and other scribes had to pass by it to return to their homes.

"Oh, there's the newcomer," Shoshana said, her voice rising with interest. "I haven't seen him before. He must be Josiah the widower, who moved here last week. Do you remember our fathers speaking about him?"

"Of course." Anna remembered, but it didn't concern her. Her father had been excited that another educated scribe had moved to the village. Josiah was the nephew of one of the village scribes, which probably helped him fit into their small community right away. She'd heard that he was already working in the vineyards.

"Although we don't really need another scribe in our village," Shoshana observed. "My father said that Levi is looking for men to join the village brigade." She paused. "He really is very handsome."

"Who?" Anna looked up at her cousin again.

"Josiah, of course." Shoshana rested a hand on her hip. "Haven't you listened to anything I've said? Come and see this newcomer."

Releasing a sigh of exasperation mixed with a small bit of curiosity, Anna put down the mantle she was embroidering and joined her cousin at the front window. A group of men walked slowly along the dusty road, heads bent in conversation. The younger students, boys of eight or so, jostled each other, some picking up rocks and tossing them off the path, while the others laughed together.

Anna knew every person's name in the village where she'd lived her whole life. She was the oldest daughter of Phanuel and Bethany, both of whom were of the tribe of Asher. But her father hadn't remarried, so Anna had taken upon herself all the household chores and obligations, including caring for her younger brother, Michael.

Michael walked among the group of students as well, and Anna knew that his bright mind made her father proud. She loved to learn as well. It wasn't a woman's duty to learn to read and write or study the law, but Anna was able to identify some letters and words. She found late-night discussions between her father and his friends fascinating. She especially paid attention to the prophecies of the Savior and wondered what changes the world would make when He came to earth. When her father sat in front of their home on warm evenings, meeting with other men of the village who came to discuss the sacred writings about the law of Moses and the psalms, Anna would settle by the window with a bit of embroidery and stitch by the light of the moon while she listened.

She picked out her brother now, who was in some sort of rock-kicking game with his best friend, David. Michael and David could pass as brothers themselves, each with their dark, curly hair and skinny arms and legs. Her gaze scanned the boys and arrived at the men. There was Shoshana's father, Benjamin, and another uncle of theirs deep in conversation. The head scribe was also among the group, and he was talking to Anna's father.

Bringing up the rear was a man Anna had never seen before. He was the only one she didn't recognize, so it must be Josiah the widower. His blue robes were simple and unadorned, and he walked with a sure step. His brown, wavy hair touched the edge of his shoulders. His profile told her he had an angular face and a short, groomed beard. Having heard he was a widower, Anna had expected him to be older, but it made sense that he was still young since he wasn't left with any children from his marriage.

He was taller than the other men, except for Levi. Her eyes flicked to Levi, who was always the tallest in any crowd. His hair was nearly black, and he had grown his beard longer than Anna preferred. He was broad shouldered and sort of lumbered when he walked. This made Anna feel like a small bird when she passed by him in the marketplace. But even though he was a large man, he was gentle. And although he was part of the village brigade—a group of men who trained each week in warfare in case they needed to protect the village from outside tribes—he'd never used his strength to intimidate women or children.

Levi rarely spoke to Anna, yet she knew he was faithful and would make a good husband. He was a shepherd by trade, so he attended the synagogue only every few weeks. He might not be like her father, an educated scribe always full of interesting conversation, but Anna thought that being a shepherd's wife would leave her with plenty of time to pursue her own love of learning.

She had already heard from more than one source that Levi intended to ask for her hand in marriage. She didn't know what he was waiting for, but she wasn't going to complain. She was comfortable in her father's home, in her routine, and besides, her father and brother needed her.

When she married, she'd move to the home of her in-laws, and she'd be under the jurisdiction of her new mother-in-law. Levi's mother was a demanding woman, if Anna were to put it kindly, and she was sure she'd be working from sunup to sundown if she married Levi. It was to be expected though, and she figured that Levi would be as good a husband as any. He glanced over at Anna's house with his dark eyes, and even though she knew he couldn't see her because of the dim interior of the room, she drew back from the window.

"Levi is taking his sweet time in asking for your hand," Shoshana said, seeming to observe Levi's glance toward the house. "If he's too slow, another man will speak for you."

Anna laughed. "Who? Unless I marry one of the old widowers. You and your sister have set your sights on all the younger men in the village." Rachel, Shoshana's younger sister, was just as much a matchmaker as Shoshana was. They constantly speculated about which man would marry which woman.

"If there's one you particularly like, we can take him off our list," Shoshana offered.

Anna shook her head with a laugh.

Shoshana tsked and started talking about the young men she had an eye out for, but Anna paid little attention because just then, Josiah the widower greeted her father. The two men grasped hands, then released their grips. Their steps slowed as they talked so that they fell behind the group.

Her father motioned toward their house as he spoke, and Anna took another step back, making sure to stay out of sight. Josiah's expression was serious, and he nodded. Seeing his full face now, Anna noticed the sadness in his eyes. This was a man who'd recently lost his wife, so of course he would be sorrowing. Anna's heart went out to him in empathy. She knew what it was like to lose a loved one.

For a moment, she wondered if he'd truly loved his wife. Had he grown up with her? Had they loved each other? What had his wife been like? Anna dispelled the thoughts from her head as her brother, Michael, burst in the front door.

"Father said I could go fishing with David," he said, scrambling across the room to grab a basket and a couple pieces of bread and cheese.

"All right." Anna smiled while she watched her brother hurry about. Fishing was his favorite thing to do.

Before he could run out the door, she snagged his arm and pulled him into an embrace. He groaned but allowed her to kiss the top of his head. "Enjoy fishing," she said.

"I will," he said and hurried to the door, his thoughts focused on one thing only. He pulled the door shut before Anna could remind him to be home in time for supper.

Anna walked into the open cooking area to straighten the baskets Michael had set askew in his haste.

"Oh my heavens," Shoshana said.

Anna turned toward her cousin.

"You have a guest."

Anna stilled. Then she looked out the window. Sure enough, her father was walking with Josiah across their courtyard. Shoshana hurried back to her cushion and took up her stitching. Anna followed, picking up the half-finished mantle. Perhaps her father and Josiah would sit outside and talk for a while, or perhaps—

The front door opened, and her father stepped inside. "Anna, there you are," he said, his gaze finding her immediately. The villagers said she took after her father, at least in appearance. He was a thin man with hair the color of cedar. His eyebrows were dark and his eyes a deep hazel, reminding her of the color of the

distant hills. In matters of scholarly study, he had a vast knowledge. In matters of practicality, he was forgetful.

"Shoshana," her father continued when he spotted his niece.
"Nice to see you here. Anna, I've invited Josiah for supper."

The man in question stepped into the house just as her
father spoke. He'd nearly had to stoop through their doorway.
Anna stood, and Shoshana rose as well.

"Josiah, this is my niece Shoshana and my daughter, Anna,"
her father said, coming into the room.

"Nice to meet you both." Josiah nodded at Shoshana, then
looked at Anna.

He was handsome, Anna admitted, but she wasn't sure how
she felt about the way he openly studied her with those dark, sad
eyes.

"Anna?" her father said.

"Oh." Her face heated up. What had her father asked? Had
he asked her something about supper? She dragged her gaze from
Josiah. "Supper will be ready by sunset."

Her father nodded and turned to Josiah. "Very well. Does
that work for you, my friend?"

"Of course," Josiah said, his voice a low timbre, filling the
small room.

The men went outside, and Anna released a breath she hadn't
realized she'd been holding. She walked to the window to watch
their progress as her father walked Josiah to the gate. Instead of
coming back inside, her father began talking to a passerby. This
was typical; he was always willing to visit with anyone.

She stood watching Josiah walk down the road until he was
out of sight.

"Anna," Shoshana said, tapping her shoulder. "Are you day-
dreaming standing up?"

Anna blinked. "Sorry. I was just thinking . . ."

Shoshana folded her arms and lifted her brows, watching
Anna expectantly. "About . . . ?"

"Josiah seems sorrowful, that's all." Anna turned from Shoshana to move into the cooking room. If they were to have a guest for supper, she would need to soak more barley. Anna also needed to harvest another pepper to make the meal that much more flavorful.

Shoshana followed her into the cooking room with a sigh. "Of course he's sorrowful," she said. "I mean, his wife died, and what man wouldn't be sad about that?" She leaned against the wall, watching Anna as she picked up the water jug.

"I wish I could help you because I'd love to get to know Josiah better," Shoshana said.

Anna wasn't fooled. The times they spent together sewing were, in fact, more of an opportunity for Shoshana to catch up Anna on the village news than for actual work.

"Did you see how the seams of his robe were frayed?" Shoshana continued to chatter. "He definitely needs a wife to sew him a new robe."

Anna hadn't noticed his robe up close. She'd noticed other things, like the broadness of his shoulders and the strong set of his jaw. Anna looked over at her cousin. "Perhaps *you* can be that wife," she said.

Shoshana laughed. "He did seem pleased when he saw me. Perhaps he likes my new tunic." She touched the line of embroidered flowers at her neckline. "You always do pretty work, Anna."

It was a compliment Anna heard frequently. She'd embroidered Shoshana's tunic, as well as a couple of Rachel's. Anna didn't mind the extra work. She liked to keep her hands busy and liked to see the delight in her cousins' eyes when she presented them with the finished work. But she was never as satisfied with her work as others seemed to be. For one thing, she unpicked her stitching frequently when she felt there was something out of place. Since her mother had taught her embroidery, Anna wanted to do it well and honor her mother's memory.

Anna knew she was pickier than most, but she wanted her work to last and her embroidery to look nice.

Shoshana flashed her a smile. "I can't wait to tell Rachel how handsome Josiah is." She reached for the bread in one of the covered baskets. "Mind if I take a couple?"

"Of course not." Anna knew there was no way to stop Shoshana from helping herself anyway.

"Thank you," Shoshana said, then opened the door that led to the back courtyard. "I'll see you tomorrow; and be prepared to tell me all the details of Josiah's tragic tale that you overhear at supper."

Anna just shook her head and waved goodbye to Shoshana. Even if Josiah did talk about his past at supper, Anna wouldn't be sharing his personal news with Shoshana or anyone else. She felt strangely protective of the man with the sorrowful eyes.

CHAPTER
SIX

JOSIAH PUSHED OPEN THE DOOR of his home—a former shepherd's hut that had been fortified. He had yet to fully set it up, and it looked like a somber place . . . echoing the recent months of his life. When his uncle had offered the use of the hut, Josiah had initially turned it down. But living in his hometown with constant reminders of his wife, Bilhah, and their infant son had only made the days and nights drag on. Bilhah had died in childbirth, and the child had died only hours afterward.

It seemed unreal that she'd been gone for nearly a year now; they'd married only two years ago. He still remembered their betrothal ceremony and the way he thought she was the most beautiful woman he'd seen when she'd stood next to him beneath the marriage huppa. If he closed his eyes, he could still see her laughing eyes and smiling mouth.

That was how Bilhah had been. Happy, laughing, always enjoying life. She also argued with him plenty and was incredibly stubborn but followed it up with her full force of love and joy. When she was first with child, she kept it a secret from no one. Almost from the moment she found out, the entire village knew.

Josiah smiled to himself as he rummaged through the handful of baskets on the table in his sparse cooking room. Bilhah had hated to cook. She'd have rather been outside talking to a friend, laughing with the children, helping an injured goat . . . She also hadn't weaved or sewn much—said it bothered her eyes. But Josiah had been fond of her, had loved being married and having someone who belonged to just him, someone who would give him children and fill his home with happiness.

The food in the baskets that neighbors had delivered was depleted. It appeared that he wouldn't be eating until supper at Phanuel's home. For a fleeting moment, he hoped the man's daughter was a decent cook, although he knew he'd eat almost anything right now. But he had to admit that being here, far away from the constant reminders of his wife, and feeling extremely hungry were better than staying in his village and being surrounded by her family members . . . and their speculation of whether he'd marry Bilhah's younger sister.

When Josiah had first heard the rumor about Bilhah's sister, he'd met with the village elders to offer his home to a young couple to rent in exchange for a donkey, a cart, and some traveling necessities. He'd said goodbye to his students, then he'd started the two-day trek toward Jerusalem.

His uncle had been surprised at first to see Josiah arrive on his doorstep but had welcomed him with open arms and had offered him a job working in the vineyards until he could become established in his true profession as a scribe. Then his uncle had brought him before the village elders, and when Josiah had told them about his education and training, Phanuel had stood and told him he would welcome another teacher.

So it seemed that God had directed Josiah's path after all. Everything had fallen into place. Although his heart was still heavy, his burden seemed lighter. Perhaps in part, his lightened burden was due to the fact that he was looking forward to a full meal for supper.

He set the baskets back in their place. A withered apple and overripe melon weren't going to get him very far, so he wandered outside and inspected the surrounding dirt patches. He supposed he should plant a garden and see to repairing the wall and gate. His uncle had told him the place had been lived in off and on but only on a temporary basis.

There was much to be done in fulfilling his duties as a new scribe, working in his uncle's vineyard, and in cleaning up his new home. Josiah appreciated the work, and staying busy throughout the day would make him too tired to brood during the long, lonely nights.

He was about to go back into the house when someone called his name from the road. He turned to see Phanuel's brother, Benjamin, walking with three women. Josiah recognized one of them as the cousin he'd met at Phanuel's home. Shoshana was her name.

"Hello," Josiah said, meeting them at the broken gate.

"I'd like to introduce my wife and two daughters," Benjamin said and proceeded to do just that. "This is my wife, Hannah."

The short woman standing next to him dipped her head, then lifted her sharp gaze to study Josiah.

The daughters seemed to take after their mother because they didn't shy away from staring at him as well. Josiah guessed they were of marriageable age. They were pretty, each of them with long, dark, wavy hair and soulful eyes. But neither of them was Bilhah.

Benjamin continued, "Shoshana, my eldest. She's a little older than her cousin Anna, who is Phanuel's daughter. And Rachel, here, is my youngest daughter, and she just turned fifteen."

Josiah nodded at the young women, and Shoshana smiled at him openly. If he were to guess, he would have thought Anna was the oldest of the cousins. She seemed more mature than Shoshana.

"Shoshana told me you will take supper with Phanuel's family tonight," Benjamin said.

Shoshana turned to her sister and whispered something. Both girls giggled.

"I am grateful for the invitation," Josiah said. "I have not quite settled in, although I'm not a skilled cook regardless."

Benjamin chuckled. "Perfect," he said. "Because we'd like to invite you to supper for *tomorrow* night."

Josiah had no reason to say no, except for the fact that he felt like an insect on a hot day being studied by a group of eager children. He hoped there wouldn't be any of the same nonsense that had occurred in his home village, where he hadn't felt like he could accept any supper invitations because they were all gatherings designed to have him interact with the daughters of the household.

Why his home village had been in a rush to see him remarried so quickly, Josiah couldn't exactly say. He wasn't a wealthy landowner or a blacksmith. He was a scribe and could eventually provide a home for a wife and family but nothing that could be considered luxurious.

"I would be honored to sup with your family," he said, knowing he couldn't turn down the invitation without being rude.

Shoshana and her sister clasped hands as if it were the best news they'd heard all day.

Josiah should have been grateful for such a warm welcome, but instead, he was feeling wary . . . and weary. "Well, I won't keep you." He gave a respectful nod to Benjamin. "I've got to get back to organizing so I can make it to supper on time."

"Yes," Benjamin agreed. "You'll soon discover that my brother's daughter is not happy if the family isn't on time for supper. She's been known to serve cold supper if her brother is late—or even withhold it completely."

Josiah forced back a smile. He found the statement quite amusing, since he knew exactly who Michael was. From his very brief observation, the boy was very bright, but he seemed to get away with a bit too much, if Josiah was being truthful. It seemed his sister worked hard to keep him in line though. "Perhaps Phanuel's daughter has good reason for that."

Benjamin blinked a couple of times as if he hadn't expected such a response.

Josiah pressed on. "Thank you again. I'll look forward to tomorrow evening."

The family stepped back from the gate, and Josiah turned toward his house. He sensed that he was still being watched, by the entire family, no less, as he reached his front door. But when he turned before entering his home, they had gone.

Walking into the dimness once again, he refilled the oil lamp, then set it by the front door so when he returned home that evening after dark, he wouldn't have to fumble around to find his way. Then he set to unpacking the final crate he'd hauled from his cart.

There were two clay jars inside that he'd wrapped with a shawl so they wouldn't break during the journey. When he lifted out the shawl, he felt a pang in his heart. The shawl had been his wife's; she'd been embroidering the edges before she'd died. She'd gotten only about halfway, and Josiah hadn't had the heart to give it away or ask someone to finish the embroidery. He remembered her becoming frustrated with the delicate stitching and pulling out the thread more than once and starting over, muttering that it would be the death of her before she'd finish the thing. It turned out that her statement had been prophetic.

He draped the shawl over the lone stool in the cooking room. Despite the memory associated with the half-finished shawl, Josiah couldn't bear to part with the garment. It also gave the place a bit more of a homey feel so it wasn't so stark inside.

He passed the rest of the time sweeping out dusty corners with a twice-patched broom. When the sun had sunk low in the horizon, Josiah brushed off his clothing, washed his face and hands from a clay bowl he'd filled with water, then set out on the path toward Phanuel's home. His stomach felt tight with hunger, and the closer he drew to the house, the more he anticipated a good meal. As he approached the now-familiar homestead, he realized he was earlier than he'd intended, but the pains in his stomach urged him on. At least he wouldn't be late.

The laughter of children coming from behind him made him slow his step, and he looked toward the sound to see a couple of boys running along the road. They were chasing some goats that didn't seem the least bothered about being chased. The boys looked to be aged five or six, but still, Josiah thought of the infant boy he'd lost. If Bilhah had lived, if their son had lived, they might have had another child, and the two brothers would have run carefree along the road like the two boys he was seeing now.

Josiah turned from the scene and continued on his trek. As he followed the final lane that led to Phanuel's home, his step slowed once again. Coming from the direction of the house were two young women. Even at a distance, Josiah could see they were Benjamin's daughters. They walked arm in arm, and the elder one carried a basket.

Had they been visiting their cousin again?

Before he could adjust his gait, Shoshana saw him. She gave him a broad smile. Josiah assumed she remembered his supper appointment.

"It's wonderful to see you again so soon, Josiah," Shoshana said.

Her younger sister simply stared at him with little apology.

"Thank you," Josiah said. "I hope you're both well."

This time Rachel smiled as well. "Oh, we are both very well." She raised her thin brows. "We were just wondering what your favorite meal is?"

At that moment, anything was his favorite meal. Cold or warm. "I'm not choosey," he said.

"Oh, you must have a favorite meal." Shoshana took a step closer. "Every man does."

Josiah stepped back. They were in public and standing on an open road, but he wasn't comfortable with these girls' boldness.

Neither of them seemed to notice his distance.

They moved forward again, their arms still linked. "You must tell us."

"Honestly, I will enjoy anything your mother prepares," Josiah insisted as he stepped around them. "I will see you tomorrow. Thank you for your concern."

"We will find out, Josiah," one of the young women said, although he wasn't sure which one had spoken, for he was striding toward Phanuel's.

He didn't look back as he reached the gate, and thankfully, he found Phanuel in the front courtyard, sitting on a low stool as he seeded a pomegranate. The man looked up from his task and smiled.

"Welcome, my friend. Have a seat." He nodded toward another stool that also sat in the shade of the pomegranate tree. "Keeping my hands busy helps me think."

Josiah could relate. He reached for a pomegranate hanging in the tree and plucked it out. Then he settled on the stool and cracked open the skin of the fruit.

"Anna will call us when supper is ready, but Michael has yet to return from his fishing excursion." Phanuel shook his head and chuckled. "If he doesn't come back soon, my daughter will have something to say about that."

"Is Michael often late for supper?" Josiah asked. In his present state, he couldn't imagine being late for any meal.

"Less now than before," Phanuel said in a conspiratorial voice. "Last week, Anna sent him to bed without supper, and that sure caught his attention. Of course, the boy was up at midnight sneaking some food, with his sister none the wiser."

"Let's hope Michael is a fast learner." Josiah added a few pomegranate seeds to the basket Phanuel was shelling them into.

"Anna's raised Michael, you know," Phanuel continued. "After the death of my wife, Anna took over without any prompting. I've been blessed. She's a fine young woman."

Josiah nodded, the ache in his heart growing sharp at the mention of Phanuel's loss. It seemed that he and Phanuel had that in common.

"Father." A voice cut into their conversation.

Josiah looked up to see Anna standing in the front entrance of the house. Her gaze met his briefly, and she appeared as if she were about to change her mind but then she said, "Have you seen Michael?"

"Not yet," Phanuel said in a knowing tone. "Josiah has come though. He wouldn't dare be late for supper."

Anna's gaze landed on Josiah again; her cheeks had pinked. It was a small thing to notice, and he wondered why he had. Although she was definitely the feminine version of her father, she looked enough like him that Josiah wondered what of her mother she had in her. Perhaps her mother had been petite? Her father was tall and thin, and Michael seemed to be growing into a sturdy young man. Yet Anna's petite frame was far from reticent. Her confidence made her seem much taller than she was.

She still wore the dark green tunic she'd had on when he'd first met her. Not that he was studying her appearance. From their first introduction, he knew her eyes were large and inquisitive, and her tunic brought out their deep hazel sharply. Her cedar-brown hair was plaited and hung over her shoulder, although several wisps had escaped and framed her face, and Josiah wondered if she was aware of the escapees. He sensed that if she were, she'd immediately put her hair to rights.

She didn't seem the type of woman to miss a thing, and instead of brushing the details of life off like his wife had, Anna seemed to relish order and . . . punctuality.

"We'll send him right in when he shows up," Phanuel told his daughter.

She gave him a brief but strained smile and said, "Thank you," then went back into the house.

When she disappeared inside, Phanuel chuckled and shook his head. Despite himself, Josiah wanted to chuckle along with Phanuel. Perhaps the man's good humor was catching.

CHAPTER SEVEN

MICHAEL CAME BURSTING THROUGH THE back door of the house just as Anna had given up on him appearing for supper and had reconciled herself to feeding only her father and his guest.

"Look what I caught." He held up his fishing basket. "From David's pond."

She peered into the basket at the three silver fish inside. "You were almost late for that? Those are pretty small," Anna said, trying to keep her voice stern, although she wanted to laugh at Michael's enthusiasm. In truth, she was relieved he'd shown up just now. She didn't want their guest to get too close of a look at the inner workings of their family.

"These were the biggest in the pond," Michael said, his eyes narrowing.

Anna tousled his curly hair. "I'm sure they were. Show Father. He'll probably want them for dessert. And tell Father supper is ready now that you've decided to show up."

Michael pulled a face, but he ran through the house and out the front door.

Anna smiled to herself as she imagined the ensuing conversation. Throughout the last little while, she'd been curious about what her father was speaking to Josiah about. They probably had a lot in common, both widowers, both scribes, but it wasn't her place to join the conversation as they seeded pomegranates in the front yard.

Moments later, Michael was back in the cooking room. "Father said to save these for tomorrow and to tell you he wants to eat in the back courtyard with our guest—Josiah."

"All right," Anna said. "Why don't you wash up while I get these fish salted?" She took the basket of fish from Michael, and he went outside again, hopefully to fetch well water to wash with.

Michael was always keeping her on her toes. But Anna was grateful for it and saw it as a blessing—to keep busy, to stay useful, and to raise a boy her mother couldn't. Her father was too lenient on him, and Anna knew it would take more than a privileged education to make a man out of her brother. He seemed to be well on his way though, even if she had to continually remind him of his manners. She knew that many times she worried needlessly about his whereabouts and activity, but she also didn't know what she'd do if something happened to him.

She filled the serving bowl with steaming barley mixed with diced peppers and onions, along with a few other spices. Earlier, Shoshana and Rachel had stopped by to inform her that they'd invited Josiah for supper tomorrow night.

"He's so somber and quiet," Shoshana had mused, watching Anna carefully. "Too serious for me. You should have seen how he didn't even smile when he was speaking to my father."

"But he's handsome," Rachel had added. "A somber and quiet husband can be good."

"Not for you," Shoshana shot back. "You'd drive him crazy with your prattle."

"You should be looking at your own reflection," Rachel retorted.

Anna had just continued mixing the batter for the date cake she planned to serve that night. She was used to the sisters bickering about men. It was comical, really, since they all knew their fathers would arrange the marriages, with their mothers' added suggestions. But without a mother, it was solely up to Anna's father, and she hadn't even voiced her opinion to him.

When Michael returned to the cooking room to proudly display his clean hands and arms, she ushered him out again with a basket of breads. By the time she started to carry out the serving dishes, her father and Josiah were in the back courtyard, arranging cushions around the outside table.

As Anna served, she tried to forget the argument between her cousins about Josiah and how he was handsome but too somber. She felt his gaze upon her a time or two but didn't pause until her father said, "We are less formal in our household since my wife passed. Anna joins us for meals."

Josiah didn't seem surprised or make a comment. In fact, his mouth softened into a slight smile as his gaze connected with hers.

His face transformed for an instant, then the smile was gone, and his sad eyes were back.

Anna found that she was staring, so she immediately turned her attention to the clay jug she was holding. She finished pouring the wine into the cups, then set the jug nearby so she could refill their guest's cup when needed.

They all bowed their heads while her father gave thanks for the food and the wine. While he prayed, Anna's mind wandered again, confirming that what Rachel and Shoshana had said was true. Josiah was a handsome man, a somber man, and they hadn't even seen him smile yet.

For a moment, the sadness in his eyes had fled, replaced by something Anna couldn't describe. But that something had warmed her heart. She felt compassion toward their guest, she decided. Compassion for a newly arrived widower in their village and compassion for a man who probably missed having a decent meal.

The men started to eat, followed quickly by Michael and herself. Anna couldn't help but notice how much Josiah ate. She filled his plate a second time, and he again gave her a nod as he thanked her.

She tried to ignore the prickle of awareness his attention brought. He was a good listener and seemed to be listening to everything her father spoke about while also observing both Michael and Anna.

Josiah hadn't spoken directly to her, except to thank her for the food, but she felt like she was getting to know him better by sharing a meal. When Michael told everyone about his three-fish catch, Josiah asked him several questions—more than Anna had ever thought to ask her brother.

She decided Josiah wasn't necessarily quiet, as Shoshana and Rachel had deemed him, but merely thoughtfully selective.

"Do you enjoy fishing over studying, then?" Josiah asked Michael.

His face flushed, and he glanced at his father before answering. "I enjoy fishing only a little bit more."

Anna smiled, and her father chuckled. "You can admit it, son," her father said. "It won't hurt my feelings."

Michael's face reflected relief, and he turned to Josiah. "I love fishing more than anything in the world."

Josiah's eyes filled with amusement. "Do you prefer fishing in a pond or a river?"

Her brother paused for a moment. "A river, I think. River fish are harder to catch so when I catch one, I feel like I won a contest."

"You have won a contest of sorts," Josiah said. "Man against fish."

Michael beamed.

Anna wanted to laugh at her brother's obvious pride. But she kept quiet while enjoying the interchange. As the only son of Phanuel, Michael certainly earned enough attention, but this attention from a near stranger was unprecedented.

"What are the best times of day to catch fish?" Josiah continued his questions.

"Right now," Michael blurted out. "Which is why I wish supper could be later."

Josiah laughed. Really laughed.

Anna stared at Josiah as his face transformed, and the sound of his laughter skittered across her skin, warming her.

"Perhaps you need to negotiate with your sister, then," Josiah continued, not even looking at her as he spoke.

But Anna felt his attention anyway.

"Now that would be a feat," her father said.

Anna raised her brows and turned to her brother, ignoring the heat creeping across her body at Josiah's mention of her. "There's another time when the fish are the most active, correct?"

"Early morning," Michael said, his shoulders slumping.

"If you awaken early enough, you can go fishing at sunrise."

She felt Josiah's gaze on her, and in a bold move, she looked over at him. Her eyes locked with his. She could tell, even without words, that Josiah approved of her counsel to her brother. She marveled that in the short time this man had been at her home, he'd relaxed and found amusement. He seemed comfortable with her small family, and for some reason, that pleased her.

"You know I can't get up early," Michael continued, his tone despondent.

Anna turned her attention to her brother. She hadn't meant to hurt his feelings. "Unless Father says otherwise, supper will still be at sunset."

Michael turned his hopeful eyes upon his father, and Anna's gaze connected with Josiah's again. A smile played on his lips, which only made Anna want to smile as well.

"I'm afraid we'll need to keep supper at sundown," her father proclaimed, giving Michael a wink. "I commend you for your effort though."

Anna sensed that Josiah was holding back another laugh. He spoke again to Michael. "Have you ever fished in the sea?"

Michael's pout faded, and his eyes rounded. "No, have you?"

"I have a few times."

All attention was now on their guest, and Josiah began to tell of his grandfather who had made his living at the Sea of Galilee.

"He fished *every* day?" Michael asked, his tone reverent.

"Almost every day," Josiah said. "I never met him because he died before I was born, so I only know what my mother told me about him."

"Is that where you're from? Galilee?" Michael pressed.

Anna could see that her father was ready to jump in, to hush Michael's questions, but he was waiting for Josiah's response.

"My mother was," Josiah said, "but when she married, she moved to live with my father."

"Was your father a fisherman too?" Michael asked.

"No," Josiah said, the sadness in his eyes returning. He reached for his wine cup and took a slow sip. "He was born with a crippled hand, and he couldn't have been a fisherman if he had wanted to. He was a learned man though, and he educated me."

"My father says you're a scribe, like him," Michael said.

Thank goodness for young, inquisitive boys, Anna thought. She'd learned more about Josiah in the past few moments than a week of village gossip had brought her.

"I am honored to be training as a scribe," Josiah said. "But I am not equal to your father. He has much wisdom, and I look forward to learning from him."

Michael's face scrunched up. "A scribe doesn't teach another scribe."

Her father chuckled. "Learning never stops, son."

Michael seemed to consider this, then said, "I know some fishing stories."

Neither her father nor Josiah discouraged Michael from taking over the conversation.

The boy came to life and eagerly discussed every fishing story and every fisherman he'd ever heard about.

Josiah listened patiently while Anna's father looked amused at Michael's eagerness. But while Josiah spoke with Michael, the sorrow in Josiah's eyes seemed to return. Anna knew he didn't have any children, but perhaps he had brothers and was missing them.

She couldn't imagine leaving her village or her family or her friends, ever. She'd been born here, and she planned to die here. Curiosity about Josiah continued to grow throughout the evening until she was wondering, quite boldly, why he'd really come to their village.

Of course, there was no way she could ask him directly, so as she served the dessert of golden-brown date cakes, she hoped her father or brother would probe into why Josiah had chosen their village after losing his wife.

But they didn't.

After Michael finished telling a tale Anna had heard multiple times, her father settled into a story that Anna had heard as well, a story that often became embellished the more wine he had in him. It was the story of his youth and how he had won many of the contests at the village festivals. He was also sure to emphasize that his studies always came before any other activities or recreation.

"Which reminds me," her father said, looking at Michael. "You need to get to studying today's lesson."

Michael groaned, but he stood up from his cushion.

"Can you first light the torches?" her father asked.

Michael lit the torches in the courtyard as the sky's orange turned violet. The night insects came out to hum and buzz, and Anna once again filled her father's and Josiah's cups with wine.

"Anna," her father said. "Thank you for the good meal."

"Thank you," Josiah echoed.

Anna nodded. "You are welcome." She rose to clear the platters of food while Michael carried the jug of wine into the house. She expected the men to remain for some time to continue talking as they nursed their final cup of wine.

She'd leave the rest of the cleanup until after Josiah departed, but she carried the platters into the cooking room. Michael had already lit the oil lamps. She cleaned the platters off and made quick work of straightening everything. She usually cleaned as she cooked, so there wasn't a lot to do following a meal.

This gave her the chance to sit at the table and continue her embroidery by the light of the oil lamps. She could hear her father's rumbling voice and tried to catch the essence of what he was saying. Josiah's responses were lower and softer, so she couldn't quite hear his words. She knew she could ask her father later what Josiah had said, but she also didn't want her father to think she was seeking too much information about their guest.

She sensed that Josiah valued his privacy and that what little he'd said about his grandfather and his parents was something he wouldn't say to just anyone. Anna treasured what he'd told her family, and she wouldn't make it a matter of village gossip.

A breeze stirred through the open windows, carrying with it the scents of the night. Anna continued to stitch, feeling at peace in her surroundings. She was grateful Josiah had come for supper. Both her father and brother had enjoyed his company, and for herself, she hoped Josiah would find the happiness he was looking for.

CHAPTER EIGHT

Josiah sat up on his sleeping mat, unable to rest. By the position of the moon that spilled its light across his makeshift bedchamber, he knew it was well after midnight. He climbed off the mat and picked up the robe he'd discarded earlier. Drawing it about his shoulders, he stepped out the back door of the tiny house.

He looked up at the night sky and its moon and starry map. Ever since returning home that evening after supper at Phanuel's home, he hadn't been able to stop thinking about Phanuel's family. First, he recalled the ease he'd felt around all the family members and then the interchange about fishing with Michael.

Phanuel had been warm and welcoming from the first time Josiah had met the man, and Josiah had felt an immediate kinship. Over the course of the meal, he'd become increasingly more comfortable.

He thought about the stolen glances he'd received from Anna. For some reason, he hadn't been bothered by her interest, unlike what he'd received from her cousins. Anna seemed open-minded and openhearted. She was very focused on her brother's well-being, and it was obvious she cared deeply for her father. These two things impressed him. Because of this, instead of pushing all thoughts of Anna to the back of his mind as he'd done with her cousins, he found himself unable to dispel them.

She'd hardly spoken to him, and he assumed it was because she was acting the demure daughter of the house, although he knew she was far from demure. She'd been very firm yet loving toward her brother and had had no trouble speaking her opinion to him.

He didn't know why all of this was running through his mind. He'd moved to get away from the memories of his wife and the pressure and expectation of marrying another so soon. Yet here he was, awake and thinking of Phanuel's daughter when he should be asleep—wondering if he'd been a good guest, if he'd thanked her enough for the meal, and if she knew how lovely she was.

Josiah rubbed a hand over his face as if he could rid himself of the image of Anna that kept coming to his mind. She was lovely, yes. But a lot of women were lovely. He'd crossed paths with plenty of them in his home village and would do so here as well. That didn't mean he needed to lose sleep over it. He very well knew he wasn't ready to remarry. He didn't know how much agony a single person could endure, but watching his wife die, followed by their precious son, was his limit.

Yet something about Anna made him want to spend more time around her. She hadn't been pushy or speculative. He knew she'd been aware of him, had listened to his every word. He'd witnessed her warming gaze when he'd laughed at something Michael had said. She'd been pleased on her brother's behalf that Michael was enjoying the company. He was a lively boy who embraced the joys of living as he looked forward to the simple things like fishing. Phanuel hadn't invited Josiah over with any expectation or ulterior motive; they'd simply enjoyed good food and good company.

Josiah trudged into the house, trying to will himself to fall asleep so he could be coherent in the morning while he labored in his uncle's vineyard, followed by teaching sessions in a room full of eager pupils. But as he lay on his mat and closed his eyes, the image of Anna and her soft-spoken words and inquisitive brown-green eyes wouldn't let him drift off.

When the night sky softened into violet and then a soft gray, Josiah rose and started his routine of prayer, then settled at the table with scrolls that contained the teachings of Isaiah—they were always a well of new insights.

But not even Isaiah could distract him now. And if there was one thing he could look forward to today, it was that he'd be sleeping deeply after the dinner with Benjamin's family.

After completing a few morning chores and eating the withered apple he'd found yesterday, he set off toward his uncle's vineyards. He arrived at the same time as the other laborers, and with little conversation, they set to work.

Once the sun hit its midday stride, it was too hot to continue working. So after a light meal with the other laborers, Josiah headed toward the synagogue, where the pupils greeted him. The collection of young boys included Michael, and they shared a knowing smile before recitations began. Josiah had no doubt that he'd be able to command Michael's attention more fully now that they'd begun a friendship.

During the rest of the afternoon, Josiah settled into the routine that was becoming familiar to him. When lessons concluded, he fell in step with Phanuel as the men and boys began their trek home.

"Anna was pleased that we ate all of her cooking last night," Phanuel said. "In that vein, she reminds me of my wife. She felt fulfilled only if her meals were completely eaten—it meant that she'd succeeded."

Josiah had had no problem eating everything Anna had served, and he was about to offer himself up as a regular supper guest but thought better of it. He was sure there would be plenty of talk circulating about him after his supper appointment at Benjamin's home tonight.

He refrained from asking anything more about Anna since Benjamin always seemed to be within hearing distance, and for good reason, Josiah didn't want his words to be misconstrued. He felt he owed Anna more respect than that.

As they neared the proximity of Phanuel's home, for a moment, Josiah wished the man would invite him to visit for a while. But that would be very presumptuous, and Phanuel was aware of Josiah's upcoming supper invitation at Benjamin's.

Besides, Josiah didn't see any sign of Anna. Not that he expected her to be in the yard, waiting for the men of her household to come home. So, he bade farewell to Phanuel. Michael had long since skipped ahead of the men with his friends and was probably fishing by now.

When Josiah reached his own place, he spent the late afternoon tilling a patch of dirt behind his house. He didn't know what to plant first, but he could at least prepare the soil. When he finished for the day, he had plenty of dirt on his clothing, so he had to change and spend extra time cleaning up, which almost made him late to Benjamin's house. When he approached the home, he knew immediately that this evening would be vastly different from the previous evening at Phanuel's home.

Shoshana and Rachel were in the front courtyard when he came up to the gate, and they welcomed him with bright smiles. As he passed by them to greet Benjamin, he could practically feel the young women staring at him.

Benjamin led him inside to a cool room with thick rugs on the floor and cushions lining the walls. "We are pleased you could join us this evening," Benjamin said with a broad smile. "My daughters have been looking forward to it all day."

A series of knots formed in Josiah's stomach, but he should have expected this turn of conversation. "Thank you for the invitation."

"A man needs a woman to cook for him, eh?" Benjamin settled on a cushion next to the low table, indicating that Josiah do the same. "It's fortunate you don't have any children to worry over."

Josiah wasn't sure how to respond, but it felt as if the breath had just left him.

"Father," someone said, coming in through the door.

Josiah turned to see one of Benjamin's daughters.

"You can't keep our guest all to yourself," the woman continued. She came to sit next to her father.

It was the younger daughter, Rachel.

"Tell us about supper last night," she continued. "What did Anna prepare?"

Now that he was faced with the question, Josiah wasn't sure that he could recall. He was too surprised by this young woman's bold nature, so different from her cousin's.

Fortunately, Benjamin came to Josiah's aid. "We can't subject our guest to so much questioning. Check on the meal preparation, Rachel."

"Yes, Father," Rachel murmured, but Josiah sensed she was secretly pleased with her ability to question him.

It wasn't long before the women joined them and two servants brought in platters of food. The meat was plentiful, and there was enough food for twice as many guests, which left Josiah wondering what other type of industry Benjamin worked.

"You remember my wife, Hannah," Benjamin said.

Hannah nodded to Josiah, and the women sat at one end of the table, while Josiah and Benjamin stayed at their end.

While they ate, Benjamin told Josiah of his oldest son, who lived on the other side of the village and ran a successful pottery trade. His name was also Benjamin. "We invited my son and his family tonight, but they are hosting a merchant from the south. My son creates beautiful pottery pieces, and he is establishing a name for himself far and wide."

Josiah mostly listened, and every so often, one of the daughters would add to the conversation. Benjamin's wife said very little, only smiled and nodded as her husband spoke and then asked the servants to do various things.

At first, Josiah was amused when Benjamin deflected his daughters' questions, but he realized it bothered him as well. It was as if Benjamin didn't value his daughters' interests or opinions. Yet Josiah was surprised at their continued boldness.

The servants came in and cleared the food and drink, another difference in the home of Benjamin versus Phanuel.

Finally, the evening came to an end, and as Benjamin walked Josiah to the gate that separated the courtyard from the road, Benjamin said, "You've likely noticed that both of my daughters are enamored of you, just as they would be with any new guest."

"I am sure they were just being polite," Josiah said. "Thank you for the meal and your kind hospitality."

"Josiah, may I be frank?" Benjamin said, placing a hand on his arm to stop his departure.

"Of course," Josiah said, not sure if he should be concerned.

"You've arrived in our village as a scribe and a widower," Benjamin said. "Naturally, there are questions. Is there any reason that you are not fit to be a husband?"

The man was direct, Josiah had to give him that. "I am still grieving over my wife, and when plans were being made in my home village for me to marry my wife's younger sister, I knew I could no longer live there. I didn't want to hurt my sister-in-law's feelings."

Benjamin was silent for a moment. "I understand. But you must also understand me."

Josiah nodded, waiting for the man to continue.

"You are eligible; fathers will approach you," Benjamin said.

Josiah exhaled. He had expected this but not so soon. He'd been in this village only a week.

"And to that end, I'd like to inquire if you've taken an interest in either of my daughters," Benjamin continued.

Not knowing what to say, Josiah rubbed at his short beard. "Both of your daughters are lovely and intelligent women," he said carefully. "I am not yet ready to replace my wife in my heart."

Benjamin's eyes narrowed, but he didn't argue. "My family will pray for your healing."

Josiah thanked the man and couldn't hurry away fast enough. It seemed that he'd left one wasp nest and stepped right into the center of another one. He strode through the dark night back to his home, thinking of Benjamin practically offering one of his daughters in marriage. What had Benjamin told his family when he'd stepped back inside his home? Had Rachel and Shoshana already had some expectation?

Josiah blew out a breath of frustration. He didn't want to offend the good people of this village. But he also needed to tread carefully. When he reached the road leading to his home, he changed his mind about his destination, and instead, he made the trek to Phanuel's home. Josiah didn't know if the man would be willing to speak with him at this hour, but Josiah knew he was in for another sleepless night if he didn't find some resolution.

When he approached the outer gate of Phanuel's home, he saw a light coming from the cooking room. The rest of the house was dark, save for the torchlight that made the edges of the back of the house glow. Perhaps Phanuel was outside and Josiah wouldn't need to disturb his children.

He opened the gate and walked around the side of the house, calling out for Phanuel.

When Josiah rounded the corner, he stopped short when he saw Anna standing there. Upon the table she stood next to sat a couple of glowing oil lamps and a set of scrolls stretched open.

Anna's eyes were huge in the glow of the torchlight, and Josiah feared that he'd startled her.

"Sorry for the intrusion," Josiah said. "I'm seeking audience with your father, if he is available."

Anna released a breath she'd seemed to be holding. "Father and Michael aren't here right now. They've gone to help Widow Tamar, whose garden caught fire."

Now that she mentioned it, the air did have a faint acrid smell.

"Will she be all right?" he asked. "Do they need help?" Here was something he could be useful at.

"Oh, yes," Anna said, seeming to breathe easier. "You needn't worry. This isn't the first time her garden has been . . . aflame. Father thinks she does it on purpose for the attention."

Josiah blinked.

Anna's cheeks flushed, and she ran her fingers over the long dark braid that hung over her shoulder. "I don't mean to gossip, but I don't want you to think you need to rush over there."

He glanced down at the scrolls on the table . . . It looked as if she'd been reading them. But, of course, she wouldn't be able to read. Village women were never taught. Perhaps she was cleaning them up.

Anna followed his gaze and placed her hand atop one of the scrolls. "You're probably wondering what I'm doing."

Josiah's mouth felt dry, and he only nodded, not sure if responding would be intrusive or rude.

"It's not a great secret," she began, "although very few know that my father taught me to read."

Josiah lifted his gaze and found himself staring at her. He noticed, although he wasn't trying to notice, that she wore a scarlet robe over her tunic. The color contrasted sharply with her dark hair yet made her look even more lovely than he remembered.

"I'm not a master of reading, by any means," Anna continued in her soft voice. "But I can get by, and my letter writing is passable as well."

Finally, he had to speak. "You can write as well?"

Instead of blushing or looking away, she smiled. "I can."

Josiah loved her smile, he realized. It made him want to smile back. Over the short time he'd been around Anna, he'd learned that her smiles weren't constant or given out freely. He was having a hard time taking his eyes off her. He was astonished that she could read and write, yes, but then again, perhaps he wasn't. Anna wasn't like any woman he'd known . . . She definitely wasn't like his wife, and she wasn't like her cousins.

She motioned toward the bench on the other side of the table. "My father will return shortly," she said. "You're welcome to wait. Unless it is something I can help you with?" Her brows lifted at her question.

And for the first time in his life, Josiah felt himself blush. Certainly it was because he felt at a disadvantage. He was standing in a courtyard, in the dark of night, with a beautiful, amiable woman looking at him, with her dark-green eyes and her skin reflecting the golden light from the oil lamps on the table.

"I—I have a matter to discuss with your father," he said, although he felt reluctant to leave. "It can wait until tomorrow." In truth, he would like to stay. Perhaps talk with Anna a little longer and discover how much she could read or find out if she'd written anything he could look at.

"I'll tell my father you came to see him," Anna said.

Was it just his imagination, or did Anna seem reluctant to send him on his way too?

"Thank you," he said, although he couldn't quite bring himself to leave.

A moment passed, and still, he did not move.

Anna tilted her head as if she just remembered something. "How was supper tonight at my cousins' home?"

Josiah hesitated. "They are very gracious, and the meal was more than I expected."

"They are generous people," she said.

He could only nod.

Anna's brow lifted slightly as if she were equally amused and wondering why he was delaying his departure.

"Thank you, again," Josiah said and gave her a final nod, then turned to walk back around the house.

Just then Phanuel arrived.

"Our guest has returned?" Phanuel said with a smile, looking from Josiah to Anna. "And I see that our secret is out."

Anna shrugged and motioned to the scrolls. "Josiah didn't seem too horrified."

Phanuel chuckled, then clapped a hand on Josiah's shoulder.

Josiah realized this was the first time he'd heard Anna say his name. His face was heating up again, so he focused on Phanuel. "I am intrigued," Josiah said.

Anna glanced away then, and Josiah hoped he hadn't hurt her feelings. He didn't know any women who could read and write, and he didn't know any who had expressed interest in the first place.

"Anna is not the typical daughter," Phanuel said as Anna rose from the table. "Leaving so soon?"

"I must make sure Michael doesn't forage the food meant for the morning meal," Anna said in a light voice. "I trust that Widow Tamar is well?"

"She is well, and happy for the attention," Phanuel said, glancing at Josiah as if they had some shared secret. "Her garden will recover, and her daughter has promised to keep a better eye on her."

"I will leave you two to talk." Anna hurried into the house.

Josiah hoped he hadn't scared her off, but he was grateful to have an audience with Phanuel.

"Have a seat and tell me what troubles you," Phanuel said once they were alone.

"You are a perceptive man." Josiah sat across from Phanuel, the scrolls strewn about the table between them.

"I have lived many years, my friend," Phanuel said.

Josiah kept his voice low as he explained what Benjamin had said, and then he included his deeper reasons of leaving his home village and the complications he'd left behind.

Phanuel remained quiet for a long moment after Josiah's lengthy explanation. "I understand your concerns," Phanuel began. "And I understand your reluctance to give any family or young woman false hope. After my wife died, there was much speculation. Time went on, and it seems that everyone now accepts my widower status. But you are young and without posterity, Josiah. Tell me, do you plan to ever marry?"

He was prepared to say no, and perhaps that would help stem the tide of speculation. He could perhaps change his mind later. But for some reason, he couldn't give Phanuel an emphatic no. "I am not opposed to marrying again . . . when I feel I can share my heart again."

Phanuel gave him an understanding smile. "It's a rare thing that a man concerns himself with his heart before marriage. That usually comes with the arrival of children and the years of living and working alongside his wife."

"I suppose it's unconventional," Josiah said. "But not impossible."
Phanuel nodded once. "Not impossible at all."

CHAPTER
NINE

"HE SAID *WHAT*?" SHOSHANA ASKED Anna as they ground wheat together on the grinding stones in Anna's courtyard. After today's task, Anna would have enough flour for a couple of weeks.

She shook her head, refusing to expound further on Josiah's visit with her father last night. She'd told Shoshana enough . . . probably too much. And that was because of her insistent prodding.

"He didn't think it was strange that you read and write?" Shoshana continued in a bemused tone. "Most men would find it off-putting."

"Josiah isn't most men," Anna said, and then she definitely knew she'd said too much.

"You're very generous where he is concerned," Shoshana said, her eyes gleaming with mischief.

"He's new to the village and doesn't deserve our censure," Anna said. "And I don't want to gossip about a sad widower." She paused. "Don't tell Rachel any of this."

"Oh, she'll hear about it without my help," Shoshana said. "Michael will say something—"

"Michael knows nothing—at least I don't think he does," Anna said. "If I can't trust *you* to be quiet, then I regret sharing it with you in the first place."

Shoshana stared at Anna, but she continued mashing the wheat kernels she was working on.

"What else did he say?" Shoshana finally said.

"I don't know," Anna said. "I went into the house."

"Hmph."

Anna released a slow breath; it seemed the questions had stopped. She was grateful when Shoshana talked about one of Rachel's interactions with another village man during market the week before.

Anna didn't want to tell her cousin that after she'd shooed Michael out of the cooking room, she'd sat by the window and listened to the men's conversation. She felt guilty about it and should probably confess to her father, but ultimately, she was glad she'd heard Josiah's words because it helped her understand him much better. Knowing that he didn't have intentions to marry, or at least any time soon, would help her as well—she could stop dwelling on his soulful eyes and rare smiles.

When he had told her father that he'd been questioned by Benjamin, Anna had been surprised, but then, perhaps the conversation was a natural progression of events. Anna didn't know if her cousins would be embarrassed to hear what their father had said. On this account, Anna didn't want to hurt her cousins' feelings. But she couldn't stop thinking about how Josiah had said he didn't want to marry and how he didn't want to offend any of the families and how her father had agreed to take his message to the village men. Benjamin would know soon enough—he might even know by now.

Surely the message would eventually trickle down to the women, and then what? Josiah would become even more fodder for gossip. On that level, Anna felt sorry for the man. Not only would some of the villagers turned their nose up at him, but he'd not enjoy continued hospitality. It was a hard thing to acknowledge, but the people of her village could forsake as easily as they could welcome.

It was at that moment, while Shoshana prattled on about Widow Tamar's habit of starting fires, that Anna vowed not to turn her back on Josiah. He would need a friendly smile and the occasional invitation to supper. Anna's own father hadn't remarried, and certainly not every man needed to remarry after losing a wife.

"Have you finished sewing your festival tunic?" Shoshana asked, bringing Anna from her thoughts.

In a couple of weeks, the village would be celebrating the arrival of spring. This was something Anna was happy to talk about. "I've finished the tunic, and this afternoon, I plan to buy the cloth for a new mantle. I'll embroider it to match the tunic."

"You are so talented," Shoshana said with a sigh. "I am sure you'll look beautiful." Then she elbowed her. "Levi will be sure to notice."

Anna pretended not to be bothered by the reference to Levi. She hadn't even thought of him for days, not since thoughts of Josiah had consumed her.

"I doubt Levi will even be at the festival," Anna said. "He's in the middle of shearing season."

"Well, someone should tell Levi that he can't miss the festival," Shoshana said. "If the woman he wants to marry outshines the other women in the village, he'll need to ask for your hand in marriage before someone else beats him to it."

"No one is going to tell him that," Anna said, her face growing hot. "Especially not you."

Shoshana just laughed, and Anna hoped her cousin wouldn't be foolish enough to speak to Levi. If a match was made between Levi and herself, it would come at the approval of her father. And so far, her father hadn't been insistent that she marry.

"Oh, here comes your father . . . and Levi," Shoshana said.

Anna snapped her head up to see the men walking along the road a short distance from the house. Sure enough, Levi was with her father. She couldn't explain why her heart sank at seeing the two of them together—she should be pleased. Yet she hadn't expected Levi to be in the village in the middle of the day when he was so busy. Had he gone to synagogue today for some reason?

She brushed the flour from her hands as her heart thudded in anticipation. She stood as the men came into the courtyard.

Searching her father's face, she tried to guess why he'd come to the house at this time of day. Was something wrong? And why was Levi with him?

"Hello, Anna," her father said. "Hello, Shoshana."

Levi nodded toward Anna. He was a man of few words, that she knew, but she would have still appreciated a greeting.

Her father turned to Levi. "I'll be back in a few moments with the goatskin tent."

Anna watched her father leave. Shoshana continued to grind the grain against the stone, but Anna stayed standing. "You're borrowing his tent?" she asked Levi.

"Your father said he never travels anymore, so he is giving me his tent." Levi shifted on his feet as if he felt uncomfortable answering her question.

"Would you like to sit on the stool, and I can bring you some water?" Anna asked.

Levi shook his head. "Your father said he'd only be a moment." His dark eyes cut from Anna to Shoshana, where she was being surprisingly quiet while she worked.

Anna noticed the softening of Levi's mouth as he watched Shoshana work. And then Anna stared at him, then stared at Shoshana, who seemed oblivious to Levi until she let escape a pink flush on her face.

"Thank you for waiting," her father said, coming out of the house. "Did you offer Levi a drink, Anna?"

"I did," Anna said quickly. "And he refused."

"Ah," her father continued. "He is a sturdy shepherd."

"This is very generous of you," Levi told her father.

"I am not in need of it any longer, so you are welcome to it," he said.

Anna knew the tent Levi used during lambing and shearing seasons was well worn, probably beyond repair. She was surprised that Levi's mother let him have a tent so desperately in need of repair.

"We will be off, then," her father told her. "I'll see you at supper."

Anna bade them farewell, and Shoshana finally spoke up, wishing them both well.

Her father walked Levi out of their courtyard, and Anna watched her cousin's eyes linger on Levi as he strode away, carrying the tent.

"*You* are interested in Levi," Anna said.

Shoshana looked at Anna in surprise. "I don't think so."

"I think so." Anna returned to the stool in front of the grinding stone. "He was watching you more than me, and you were blushing."

At this, Shoshana's face colored again. "I wasn't blushing, and he wasn't watching me."

Anna folded her arms, keeping her gaze steady. "I know what I saw."

Shoshana threw her hands up. "What am I supposed to do? Everyone knows that Levi is intended for you. Even Levi knows it."

"Levi hasn't asked my father for my hand in marriage," Anna said. "And now that I've seen the way he looks at *you*, I'm going to speak to my father. I'm not going to marry a man you care about, and it's plain Levi is interested in you—even if he hasn't admitted the truth to himself. I don't care what the village gossips might say."

To Anna's surprise, Shoshana's eyes filled with tears. She wiped at her face quickly as if she could possibly conceal the fact that she was crying.

"Shoshana, what is it?" Anna asked, kneeling by her cousin.

"My father will never let me marry a shepherd," Shoshana said in a tight whisper. "He might consider someone as poor as Josiah only because he has the noble profession of a scribe and will eventually rise in rank and status."

Anna rocked back on her heels. It was clear that she hadn't entirely thought through what it might mean for Levi to ask for

Shoshana's hand. "Even if that's the case, why have you continually encouraged me about Levi?"

Shoshana swiped at her face. "Because he deserves a good woman."

Anna wrapped an arm about her cousin. "Levi's a good man, and I agree that he deserves a good woman. Have you spoken to your parents?"

Shoshana shook her head.

Anna felt the weight of Shoshana's discouragement as if it were her own. Her cousin might be a bit outlandish at times, but she was still family, and her heart was breaking. "How about I talk to my father?"

"No," Shoshana said immediately, pulling away from Anna. "He'll tell my father, and then I'll be mortified because I know what my father will say. I've heard him make enough disparaging remarks about shepherds and their simple ways."

"My father can be trusted," Anna insisted. "He won't say anything to your father if you don't want him to. But it might give us some more information instead of just assuming your father would be against such a union."

Shoshana went quiet for a moment. She wiped at her eyes again, then said in a trembling voice, "All right."

CHAPTER
TEN

THE WEEK PASSED BOTH SLOWLY and quickly for Josiah. Slowly, because Phanuel had invited him for the Sabbath evening meal, which he was very much looking forward to, and quickly, because he hadn't had a spare moment to relax. In addition to working in his uncle's vineyard each morning, Josiah had prepared his garden plot and repaired his broken gate. He'd also scrubbed the interior of his small house, making it into a decent yet humble home.

The afternoon before Sabbath eve started, lessons at the synagogue concluded early so everyone could go home to make their Sabbath preparations. Josiah hoped to make it to the market before the final stalls closed so he could find some seedling starts. His wife had done all the gardening during their short marriage, so he also hoped someone could give him advice on where to begin.

"Josiah," someone called behind him before he could escape the synagogue.

He turned to see Benjamin coming out as well. "Thank you for your excellent contributions," he said.

Josiah should have felt warmed by the compliment, but instead, he felt only wary. And he was justified in the very next moment.

"Have you thought more about our conversation the other week?" Benjamin asked.

Josiah didn't have to ask Benjamin to clarify what he was speaking of. He took a deep breath and said, "I have been thinking about it, and I can tell you that I'm not ready to marry again, especially so soon after moving here."

Benjamin blinked, as if he were surprised, but then he gave a hearty chuckle. "You may change your mind at the festival once you see the women in all their finery."

Josiah wanted to protest, but he knew it would be useless.

Benjamin leaned forward to speak in a low voice, as if they were surrounded by inquisitive people, when, in fact, they were the only ones remaining in the synagogue. "Shoshana would make an excellent match for you. She will be kind and understanding of your loss."

Josiah opened his mouth, then shut it again because Benjamin didn't wait for an answer.

"Happy Sabbath, Josiah," Benjamin said as he moved outside.

Josiah followed, but the man seemed to be in a hurry. It was just as well because Josiah still had to try to make it to the market before everything closed down. He walked toward the village center, greeting several people along the way. He'd been living here for only a few weeks, but already he was starting to get to know his pupils and their families.

As he neared the market square and saw only a couple vendor carts remaining and that those were being packed up, he knew he was too late. He would now most likely have to wait a few more days before planting anything in his garden plot. One vendor waved him over. "Are you in need of barley?" he asked, holding up a sack. "I've some left."

Josiah strode over. Barely soup was better than nothing. "I'll take a week's portion," he said.

The man bent to measure out the amount, and after Josiah paid him, he turned to continue through the square as he made his way back home. Two women walked toward him. Not exactly toward him but in his direction. It took him a moment to realize it was Anna and her cousin, Shoshana.

"Hello, Josiah," Shoshana sang out.

"Hello," Josiah said and stopped there. Anna was looking at him, her eyes curious, her expression open and friendly. She wore a white mantle over her head, contrasting with her dark, wavy hair. Shoshana also wore a mantle, and Josiah assumed it was what both women wore in the public market.

"You arrived quite late at the market," Shoshana continued in a teasing voice. "Is there something you were looking for? Perhaps something to take to your Sabbath supper with Anna's family?"

Anna threw a stern glance at her cousin as if she didn't approve of Shoshana's bold questions.

Josiah decided to humor her, and he lifted the sack of barley. "I found some barley, although I'm sure Anna has plenty of it herself. I came here hoping to find seeds to plant a garden. It seems that my neighbors have quite the head start on me."

"Seeds?" Anna said. "What do you want to plant?

Josiah was surprised to have Anna asking the questions now. He hesitated. "I'm not sure. I was hoping someone could give me advice as to what to plant this late in the spring. I'm afraid that my wife took care of all the gardening." He stopped, wondering why he'd brought up his wife. It had felt like a normal thing to say too. He waited for the sharp jolt of pain, but it didn't happen, and Anna didn't seem off-put by his reference.

"Anna can tell you all about what to plant," Shoshana said.

Anna shot her cousin another sharp look, but Shoshana seemed oblivious.

"Come with us," Shoshana said. "We'll show you Anna's garden, and she can tell you what you should be planting now."

Despite the invitation, Josiah didn't move. He looked at Anna. The invitation should come from her. She met his gaze and nodded. "I have some time before I need to start meal preparations. You're welcome to come see our garden, and I can give you some advice."

Shoshana smiled. "Don't be fooled by Anna's modesty. She's an expert gardener, an excellent cook, and she can embroider better than anyone I know."

Anna's cheeks flushed.

Josiah wanted to smile, but he wasn't sure if he should. "Is there anything Anna does poorly?" he asked, mostly speaking to Shoshana yet keeping his gaze on Anna.

"If there is, I haven't witnessed it," Shoshana said.

Anna's cheeks only flushed more.

"I wouldn't mind some gardening advice," Josiah said, trying to steer the conversation.

"All right," Anna said, darting a glance at Shoshana. "We can go there now."

So the three of them walked toward Phanuel's house. Shoshana chattered, and Josiah found that he wasn't paying particular attention to what she was saying. He was required only to nod every so often. He was much more interested in Anna's actions, and for the most part, she kept silent, letting her cousin take over the conversation.

At the gate of Anna's house, Shoshana said, "Oh, I just remembered. I need to help my mother because my brother's family is coming to Sabbath supper. I'll see you both later."

Before Josiah could decide if it was right and proper for him to be spending time with Anna alone, Shoshana left the both of them.

"Well," Anna said, looking up at Josiah with an amused expression. "I guess we're on our own."

Even though they'd only been walking, Josiah realized his heart was racing. "Is your brother or father at home?"

"Michael is already fishing, and my father will be home shortly," Anna said. "There are a few people he visits regularly just before Sabbath. He is looking forward to you joining us at our meal tonight."

Josiah couldn't look away from Anna's eyes, and he wasn't sure that was a good problem to have. "Perhaps you can show me the garden when I return for supper," he said. He'd spent a short time alone with Anna when he'd found her reading scrolls, but this—this felt different and made him nervous.

"I can give you some cuttings and bulbs if you come with me now," she said. "Then you can plant them before supper and get a good start on your garden."

It was an invitation he'd be foolish to refuse. "I'd like that."

Anna turned from him and opened the gate to the front yard. Josiah followed as they walked around the house, past the back courtyard where he'd found Anna reading the other night, and past a pen with chickens and two goats to a well-tilled garden. Young shoots of plants were protruding from the rich soil on one end of the garden, and on the other end, more mature plants grew tall.

Josiah gazed at the garden, feeling overwhelmed. The time and care that went into this garden was plain, and he didn't know if he had enough time, even though the days were getting longer with the approaching summer.

"You look lost," Anna said gently.

Josiah looked over at her. She didn't know how true her words were, in more ways than one. "I don't even know where to start."

Anna placed her hands on her hips and tilted her head. "Let's start with three things so you can get comfortable with caring for a smaller number of plants."

"All right," he said. "I don't know enough to contradict your advice."

Anna smiled as if she found that amusing—had it been amusing? "I'll fetch some baskets, and then you can help me dig." Her gaze moved down the length of his body. "Are you worried about getting dirt on your clothing?"

"Not if you aren't," he said.

Anna laughed.

Maybe he was humorous. It was rare that he found humor about anything—who would have thought it would be over a simple conversation about gardening?

Anna left him to continue admiring the thriving garden. The breeze picked up, bringing with it the scents from the goat pen. A bleating caught his attention, and he walked over to where a couple of scruffy goats had stuck their heads over the railing.

"Hello, there," Josiah said, scratching one of the she-goat's heads. She was obviously heavily pregnant.

"You probably need a goat too," Anna said, coming out of the house, carrying several baskets.

Josiah looked up at her. "I, uh, I don't mean to come over here and raid everything you have." As she approached, he reached for the baskets and took them from her. "I suppose fresh milk would be nice once in a while."

Anna smiled and shook her head. "You're a peculiar man, Josiah." She walked past him, picked up a small, rough-hewn shovel, and right there, at the edge of the garden, she knelt in the dirt. "Two of our goats are pregnant, and I'm sure my father would be pleased to give you one of the kids."

Josiah picked up another shovel near the garden and knelt beside Anna. "You are very generous, and I appreciate it. Helping with my garden is more than I expect in the first place. I don't want to put your family out."

Anna didn't say anything for a moment as she dug around a plant. Josiah just watched her as he waited for instructions. When she got deep enough in the dirt, she said, "Slide a basket right next to the base and help me lift this out. We want to keep as much of the roots intact as we can."

Josiah grabbed the nearest basket and set it in the hole next to the root bulb. Anna placed her hands on either side of the bulb, and Josiah shifted so that he was across from her and could use his hands to more fully support the clump of dirt. Together they lifted and set the entire thing in the basket.

Anna sat back on her heels and brushed the dirt from her hands. "When we get to your house, we can separate this plant and create several starters."

He brushed his hands off too, then moved with Anna as she dug up another plant on the other side of the garden. This time, she let him do most of the digging, and once again, they lifted it out together.

Once they had four baskets loaded with plants, Anna declared that they were finished for now. She rose to her feet, and Josiah joined her, brushing off his clothing. He picked up all four of the baskets, and said, "Can I borrow one of your shovels?"

Anna brushed the hair back from her braid that had fallen out of place. "Sure, and I'll come with you and help you plant."

Josiah realized he was staring at her without answering. "Do you have time?" He glanced at the horizon. The sun was only a couple of hours from sundown, and Sabbath started at sundown.

"The two of us will make the work light," Anna said with a shrug, then she picked up the shovels they'd been using.

They walked to Josiah's house, and he was grateful they didn't encounter Benjamin or anyone in his family. Josiah didn't relish the thought of starting any village gossip about how much Anna was helping him. He just enjoyed being in her company and would hate for rumors to circulate and taint their growing friendship.

These thoughts caused him to wonder if it were possible for an unmarried man to have a genuine friendship with an unmarried woman. He supposed it happened sometimes, at least he hoped. He very much enjoyed spending time with Anna. She seemed to listen carefully to what he said, and she was also quick to provide solutions to his growing litany of challenges.

CHAPTER ELEVEN

ANNA HADN'T INTENDED TO BE nosy, but Josiah seemed to be opening up the more time she spent with him. They, indeed, had made quick work of planting the garden that hadn't looked like a garden at all when they'd started. It was plain that he'd put some effort into preparing the soil, but looking around the small yard and the outside of the house made it clear to Anna that the place had been neglected for years.

When they had transferred the plants, Anna piled the baskets together and straightened. "It looks like you have a lot of work ahead of you," she said, waving toward the house. "Is it in good repair inside?"

Josiah lifted his brows as if he were surprised at her question. Perhaps it was a bit bold.

"I'll admit that I've mostly been cleaning since I arrived," he said. "I didn't expect much, especially when first getting settled." He released a sigh. "I've made some progress for a lone man."

"Hmm," Anna said, her eyes brightening. "I'd hate to see what this place looked like before you did all the work you say you've done."

Josiah laughed. The sound was unexpected. "Are you questioning my skills?" he asked, still smiling.

"No, I trust you," she said, returning the smile.

He knew she was speaking mostly in jest, but the statement did something strange to his heart. It was like the sun had just come out after several cloudy days.

"I'll take these back," she said, moving to retrieve the baskets.

"I'll bring them when I come for supper," he said. "Don't worry about carrying everything back."

Anna hesitated, her gaze connecting with his. "All right. Don't be late." Her voice was firm, but her eyes were smiling.

"I wouldn't dream of it," Josiah said, holding back his own smile. When she left, he hurried into the house and retrieved a length of cloth he used for bathing. He made his way to the small stream that meandered behind his homestead and washed, dried, and returned to the house to dress in clean clothes.

He sat at the small table in the cooking room and cleaned his fingernails that had taken in their share of dirt. While he worked, he glanced across the room at the mantle that hung over the second chair he'd been able to procure. His wife's clumsy embroidery stitches on the mantle might not create the most appealing article of clothing, but since she had done it, he valued it.

Now, looking at the mantle didn't bring the usual wave of misery he felt. He'd had a good day, a busy and fulfilling day. He'd laughed, he'd smiled, he'd worked hard, and he was looking forward to another decent meal prepared by Anna.

Fingernails clean, he reached for the fabric. It was of good quality and well-woven, and he turned it over in his hands. His wife might be gone, but she was still a part of his heart. Today had been the first day he'd been able to speak of her in such a casual setting as he had at the market with Shoshana and Anna.

And it didn't pain him to touch the mantle that his wife used to hold while she attempted to embroider. Curious, Josiah turned it over only to see a series of knots on the backside. For some reason, the sight of them made him chuckle. He remembered Bilhah specifically complaining about how her mother had told her that embroidery should look beautiful on both sides of the cloth—reflective images of each other.

Josiah ran his fingers over the knots his wife had tied. He waited for the ache to grip his chest, for the tears to burn his eyes. But he only smiled at the memories. Something in his heart had lightened. The clumsy stitches were endearing, and for a moment, he wanted to show the mantle to Anna and tell her about his wife's aversion to stitching.

He wondered if Anna sewed. Well, of course she did. Shoshana had mentioned it, and every living woman sewed, but he wondered if Anna *liked* to sew. How skilled at embroidery she really was. A wild thought entered his mind before he could stop it. What if he asked someone—someone like Anna—to finish the mantle?

No, that was a ridiculous idea. This mantle was personal. It was something that only he knew about—he wanted to keep the half-finished shawl a memory between his wife and him.

With a sigh, he spread it across the table, knots and all. Then he pulled on his outer robe and left his house. Picking up the baskets and shovels, he set off along the road. The sun had nearly set, and the streets were quiet. It seemed that everyone was inside preparing for Sabbath.

The glow of the torchlights welcomed Josiah to Anna's home. He knocked on the front door, and Michael answered.

"You're here," Josiah said, and Michael grinned.

"If I was late for Sabbath supper, my sister would definitely kill me."

"I heard that," a female voice called out from somewhere within the house.

Josiah chuckled.

"Let's go around the side of the house, where father is," Michael said, pulling the door shut and effectively blocking Anna from hearing any more of their conversation.

Josiah was sure Michael had used that technique more than once to escape his sister's censure.

When they walked into the back courtyard, Josiah saw a table set with cups, bowls, and plates. In the center sat the candles that would be lit right before the meal. Josiah joined Phanuel and Michael at the table, all the while wondering where Anna was. He didn't have to wonder for long because moments later, she came out the back door, carrying a platter of meat and steamed barley. She nodded to Josiah but didn't say anything before she went back into the house to fetch another dish of sliced fruit.

Once they began the meal, Phanuel discussed some of the business of the synagogue, as well as a few of the older students. Since Josiah taught the younger students, he didn't know the individual boys whom Phanuel was speaking about. Josiah was impressed with how Anna seemed to know each of the families and how she offered up her opinion.

Anna was also an excellent hostess, making sure no one's cup or bowl emptied. More than once, Josiah had to pull his attention away from watching Anna refill a cup to focus on Phanuel's conversation.

Josiah ate until he was more than full. It seemed he'd outlasted Phanuel and Michael. When Phanuel leaned back with a satisfied expression and said, "Thank you, the meal was excellent," Josiah couldn't agree more.

Phanuel then cast a pointed look at his son, and Michael dutifully spoke up. "Thank you, Anna."

Josiah couldn't help but smile. Something about being around Michael brought him joy. In fact, he didn't remember smiling this much in a single day for a long time. He glanced over at Anna and found that she was looking at him.

"I agree with both your father and brother," Josiah said. "The meal was excellent, and I appreciate the invitation."

"You're all welcome," Anna said, looking quickly to her father as if she were avoiding Josiah's direct gaze.

But Josiah didn't miss the color in her cheeks. Was it because of his compliment? Or was it something else? He suddenly wanted to know, but he was chastising himself too. He had left his village to stop the constant speculation and pressure about marrying again, yet here he was causing another woman to blush.

"Will you stay for our study?" Phanuel asked Josiah.

Josiah knew he couldn't say no. He was curious about how their family studied the sacred writings and whether Anna would participate since he knew she was learning to read.

"Of course," Josiah said.

Phanuel rose to his feet. "I'll fetch the scrolls." He carried out a couple of remaining platters on the way into the house, and Anna refilled each cup, then went into the house as well, carrying the jug.

"Will you come fishing with me?" Michael asked when they were alone.

"Which day did you have in mind?" Josiah asked, finding that he very much appreciated the invitation from Michael.

"Tomorrow after the sun sets," Michael said. "My father and sister won't let me fish beneath the moonlight, but David says that the fish are hungry then. Maybe my father would let me try it if I were with you."

"What if your father wants to take you?" Josiah asked, hoping he wouldn't be intruding on a family decision.

"He tells me that after supper, he doesn't have the strength to walk all over the village."

"Now what are you trying to talk poor Josiah into?" Anna said, coming into the courtyard. She carried a small basket and set it on the table.

"Nothing," Michael said.

Anna crossed to Michael and placed her hand on his shoulder. "I think I can guess . . . Does it have to do with fishing?"

Michael ducked his head, and Anna smiled. She looked at Josiah, and it was like they shared an unspoken conversation.

Anna took her seat and rifled through her basket. She lifted out a piece of cloth and thread. Josiah realized she was about to embroider. He couldn't help but watch her as she turned the cloth toward one of the oil lamps on the table to get more light. Then she began to stitch.

From his position, Josiah could already see the violet and blue pattern emerging on the linen cloth. "What are you making?" he asked before he could stop himself.

Without looking up, she said, "I'm embroidering Shoshana's mantle that she wants to wear to the festival. She tells me that I'm a much faster seamstress than she—I think she's just trying to get out of work."

Josiah nodded. "Shoshana sounds like a clever woman. Do you often take on projects for her?"

Anna looked up then, and Josiah gazed into her eyes that were filled with amusement. "As a matter of fact, I do," she said. "I suppose I am a very nice cousin."

"Shoshana is always at our house," Michael said. "Sometimes I think she lives here."

"Michael," Anna said as if she were censuring him, but her smile gave her away. "Tell me about these fishing plans you made with Josiah."

Josiah warmed at the way she'd mentioned him in her request to her brother.

Michael squirmed a little before answering, but then Phanuel came out of the house.

"Apologies for my delay," he said. "I had to search through my scrolls to find these particular ones." He held up a batch of papyrus scrolls. Sitting, he spread them out one by one. "I thought we could read Isaiah's prophecies tonight."

"The ones about the special servant?" Michael asked.

Josiah was impressed with the eagerness in the boy's voice.

"Here we are," Phanuel said. "We'll continue with Isaiah's prophesies about the coming King."

"Would you like to read for a while?" Phanuel asked Anna.

She didn't seem surprised at the request. She set down her stitching and reached for the scroll. After a slight pause, she began to read. "'For unto us a child is born, unto us a son is given. And the government shall be upon his shoulder. And his name shall be called Wonderful, Counsellor, The mighty God, The everlasting Father, The Prince of Peace.'"

Josiah had never heard the scriptures read in a female voice, and the words struck him anew. They were softer somehow, gentler, and even more humble. As Anna read the words he was so familiar with, it felt as if he were hearing them for the first time. Or perhaps gaining a deeper understanding.

"Thank you, Anna," Phanuel said when she finished. "Do you have any thoughts about what we read before we continued?"

Anna smiled, looking down at the scrolls and not speaking for a moment. When she finally spoke, her tone was reverent. "I find myself thinking frequently of what the world will be like with the coming of the Messiah. Will governors and kings praise Him? Will men lay down their weapons and allow peace to reign?" She lifted her gaze, and her eyes seemed to shine. "I wonder if He will be born in our lifetime or perhaps our children's lifetime. That possibility makes me want to always stay true to my faith."

Phanuel rested his hands on the table and linked his fingers together. "We can't know exactly when the Savior will come, but I agree that we must be prepared. Thank you for those thoughts, Anna." Father and daughter exchanged smiles, and then Phanuel turned to Michael. "Ready to read, Michael?"

Michael began. "'Of the increase of his government and peace there shall be no end, upon the throne of David, and upon his kingdom, to order it, and to establish it with judgment and with justice from henceforth even for ever.'"

When Michael finished, the family discussed what some of the verses meant. Josiah shouldn't have been surprised that Anna continued to participate fully in the discussion.

"Excuse me?" a woman's voice interrupted the conversation.

Josiah looked over to where a woman had entered the back courtyard. He didn't know her, but that wasn't unusual.

"My mother, Tamar, has fallen," she continued, her voice trembling. "Her leg is twisted, and she hit her head too. We've already sent for the healer, but I am very worried about her."

Both Phanuel and Anna rose to their feet. "We will come right away," Anna told the woman.

Phanuel nodded, then looked at Michael. "Go ensure the healer is coming," he said.

"Can I help with something?" Josiah asked.

"Come with us," Phanuel said without hesitation.

Josiah followed the three of them out of the courtyard. He knew this woman named Tamar was the one who had set her own garden on fire. Although he had never met her, he hoped there was something he could do. His heart went out to her daughter.

Tamar's home wasn't far, and Josiah went with the others into the small gathering room. He immediately sensed the somber atmosphere, and dread knotted in his stomach. Before he even saw the woman laid out on a rug in the center of the room, he sensed that her time was short.

Tamar was lying with her eyes closed. She wasn't moving, but the shallow rise and fall of her chest indicated that she was breathing. The woman's forehead had been wrapped with strips of linen, but blood had seeped through. Someone had covered her with a blanket, concealing whatever had happened to her leg.

Anna knelt by the woman and picked up her hand, and Phanuel went to her other side.

"Tamar," Anna said in a gentle voice. "It's Anna. Can you hear me?"

There was no response.

Phanuel placed his fingers on the side of Tamar's neck. After a few silent moments in which everyone seemed to hold their breath, Phanuel looked up. "She is very weak. Pray that the healer arrives soon."

Tamar's daughter let out a sob and covered her mouth. Her shoulders shook as she cried, and although Josiah felt completely helpless, he wished he could comfort her. Anna continued holding Tamar's hand, and Phanuel rose to open the door when someone knocked. Michael entered, and with him was the healer.

The healer was a man not much older than Josiah, and he went right to work without speaking to anyone. First, he removed the linen wrap and examined the wound. He asked for another strip of cloth to rebandage her head. The daughter was quick to locate one.

Next, the healer lifted the blanket to examine the woman's leg. Her foot was twisted and her ankle swollen. It was a bad injury.

"We will wait to treat the ankle," the healer said. "The truth is that I don't think she'll survive the night because of her head injury."

Tamar's daughter sank to the floor.

The healer opened a satchel he'd brought and took out a pouch of incense that he set up and began to burn. The room filled with the pungent smoke, the same type of incense that had been used when Josiah's wife had gone into labor with their child.

The scent made Josiah feel sick, and he was bothered once again that he couldn't do something for this woman who was beloved by her neighbors and her daughter. In that moment, all he could do was remember the death of his wife and how miserable he was without her.

Anna rose to her feet and pulled Tamar's daughter into her arms.

Phanuel rose as well and came to stand next to Josiah. "I don't think there's anything more we can do now. Why don't you see Michael home? I'll be there shortly."

Josiah didn't want to admit it, but he was more than happy to leave this house of mourning.

Michael was quiet on the way back to the house, and Josiah knew he didn't have many words of comfort to offer.

He and Michael cleaned the rest of the table in the back courtyard, and by the time that was done, Phanuel had returned.

He pulled Josiah aside and said, "Anna will remain the rest of the night with Tamar and her daughter. I don't expect the woman to hold on much longer. Thank you for your help tonight."

Josiah had done nothing, but he nodded anyway. Beneath the moonlight, he walked back to his house, feeling that all the joy and light of the day had just been extinguished. He hated that he'd been so useless. He didn't like being so weak.

CHAPTER
TWELVE

ANNA HADN'T SEEN JOSIAH SINCE the day of Tamar's burial. She knew he'd come only because he'd been with the family the night of her death. Otherwise, he would have had no obligation to a woman he'd never met in life. Anna had been worrying about him, and now she stood at the window, watching the men walk home from the synagogue.

Again, Josiah wasn't with the main group. She wondered if he'd been delayed or had walked a different route. She also wondered if he was avoiding her for some reason. It didn't really make sense for him to do so, but it would explain why he hadn't even spoken to her except for a single greeting at the funeral.

Yet Josiah and Michael had gone fishing a few nights ago. Michael had had to promise to do extra chores to get their father to agree to him staying out late, but their father trusted Josiah a great deal. Michael had talked excitedly about the fishing expedition for the next two days. However, Anna didn't feel like she could very well probe Michael for more information than he'd already given up.

She didn't like to leave things unsaid between her and Josiah, but she supposed he was probably unaware of her constant thoughts. He was likely living his life with no thought to the turmoil she was going through. She wanted to know how his garden was faring. She wanted to know if he had settled in. She wanted to know if he was all right—being in the room with the dying Tamar couldn't have been easy.

Perhaps she was letting all this bother her because Shoshana and Rachel were visiting an aunt in the neighboring village, and Shoshana wasn't around to distract her. She turned from the window and greeted Michael as he ran into the house. "I'm going fishing with David, and Father said I could!"

Anna smiled to herself but turned a stern eye on her brother. "What time will you be home?"

"In time for supper," he said, scurrying past her.

She grasped his arm before he could get very far. "In time for what?"

"In time to clean up *before* supper," he said.

"That's better," Anna said and leaned down to kiss the top of his head.

He groaned and dashed away.

Anna laughed. She knew that someday he'd be too old for such interactions, so she cherished each one now. With Michael out of the house and her father settled in the front yard, speaking with a villager, Anna decided she'd take a walk. She picked up a basket and put in a few small loaves, then covered them with a cloth. Perhaps she'd pay someone a visit, perhaps not. She would begin her walk and decide from there.

She bade farewell to her father, who barely looked up from his conversation, and she set off along the dusty road. The weather was overly warm today, and the late afternoon brought a dry heat, making her wish she'd thought to bring a goatskin of water.

Slowing her pace as she approached Josiah's small homestead, she decided she'd been foolish to come all this way to check on a man who probably hadn't thought about her. Or who had other things to worry about. So she decided she'd continue past the homestead and not knock on his door.

But she paused when she spied Josiah behind the house, work-ing in the garden. Well, *working* might not be the most accurate description. He seemed to be single-handedly destroying it. He stood over his cultivated rows, chopping at the earth as if he were trying to kill rodents. Perhaps he'd had an infestation of some sort?

Before she could think better of what she was doing, she opened the gate and rushed to the garden. Josiah's actions slowed when he saw her, and his eyebrows shot up. Up close, she saw that his forehead was damp and his clothing showed perspiration stains.

"What are you doing?" Anna asked.

He wiped his forehead with the back of his hand. "There are hundreds of beetles, and they're eating the plants faster than I can destroy the pests."

Anna didn't have to walk into the garden to see one of the beetles hop up on a leaf as if to prove Josiah's point. "Do you have any wine?" she asked.

"Yes . . ." He looked more confused than ever. "I can fetch you some cool water from the well if you're thirsty."

Anna would have laughed if he didn't look so serious. "The wine is for the beetles. We will put a few cups of it in your garden to attract the beetles. They will climb in, drink their fill, then drown."

Josiah didn't say anything for a moment, just stared at her as if he were deciding whether to believe her. Then he stuck the shovel into the dirt, brushed off his hands, and stepped out of the gar-den. "It's not high-quality wine," he said. "Are the beetles finicky?" Anna smiled at him, and he smiled back. The change in his coun-tenance was remarkable. She wanted to tell him that he should smile much more often, but perhaps she'd save that comment for later. "I guess we'll find out," she said.

"I'll be out in a moment," he said. "I don't think my house is ready for public viewing just yet."

Anna nodded and waited as he went into the house. She wasn't ready to see something so intimate as the inside of his home either, no matter how unassembled it might be. With only the two of them, it was improper, even if they were just fetching wine to kill beetles with.

Josiah returned with a small jug and several clay cups. He poured the wine into the cups, and Anna distributed them about the garden. "I hope you weren't saving the wine for a special occasion."

"No, I bought it for last Sabbath," he said, "but I didn't have any company to share it with, so there is plenty."

That is good news, Anna thought. Not that he didn't have any company and spent his Sabbath alone, but that he wasn't prone to drinking in excess. They both stood back to watch the beetles. For a while, the beetles didn't seem to take an interest, then a couple of them made their way to one of the cups.

"It's working," Josiah said.

"Did you doubt me?" Anna said, glancing over at him.

"No, but to see it in action is amazing." His gaze connected with hers. "You have helped me in many ways, Anna. Thank you."

His gratitude was simple and sincere.

"Thank you for taking Michael fishing at night," Anna said. "It was all I heard about for days." She didn't ask her other questions about why she hadn't seen him, because she knew they'd sound petulant. Besides, she knew he couldn't just show up at her house, not without an invitation from her father or even her brother.

"I'll fetch you some cool water," he said. "It's rather hot today."

"All right." Anna didn't feel in a hurry to leave, and Josiah was definitely in need of water. While she waited for him, she checked on her basket of bread. If she gave him the basket, he'd know she'd been coming to his house directly and not merely passing by when she'd seen him in the garden.

She took a deep breath, trying to decide what to do. By the time he returned, she'd determined to complete the initial intention of her errand.

He handed her a cup of cool water, and she sipped at it while he drank down his entire cup.

"I brought you some bread," she said after he finished. She handed over the basket. "I didn't know if you bake."

"Very poorly, but I'm getting better," Josiah took the bread and bit into it right then and there. "You are spoiling me."

For some reason, that comment made her feel warm all over. "I hope I'm not intruding on your privacy."

Josiah didn't brush off the comment like she'd thought he might. "You are not intruding, Anna. I hope you'll never feel that way, but I also don't want you to feel that you have to provide for me. I am nearly on my feet now." He waved to the garden. "I've even learned to trick the beetles."

Anna nodded. "You will soon be completely independent and won't need my help."

Josiah set the roll back in the basket and re-covered it with the cloth. "I don't know if I would go that far," he said. "But I don't want you to feel like you have to keep helping me. I should be looking for ways to help you and others in the village instead of always being on the receiving end. I even thought about joining the village brigade, but I've been told scribes are exempt."

"That's true," Anna said. She knew the village brigade had stood up to raiders from time to time. One raider had even been killed a few months ago. It made her shudder to think of such violence so close to home. In the main city of Jerusalem, soldiers were present to keep the order, but the soldiers didn't bother helping the outlying villages.

The scribes of the village were exempt from serving because their education was valuable and couldn't easily be replaced. Besides, it seemed that Josiah had trouble gardening, let alone wielding a weapon against a raider.

She hid a smile, but something was bothering her. Was Josiah brushing her off with all his talk of becoming more independent from those serving him? Surely, she wasn't the only person to bring him food and offer help. Perhaps it was overbearing to him after so many weeks. "I am sure once you get your house and garden in order, you'll have more time to look for ways to help others," Anna said in a light tone. "I best be on my way. I hope your garden can be salvaged."

She turned to go but was surprised when Josiah reached out and grasped her arm. He let go immediately, but it was enough to make her pause and turn back to him.

"I'm saying everything badly," Josiah said. "For all the scholarship I can claim, I am not talented at conversing . . . with certain people."

Anna's surprise didn't fade. "Certain people?"

"Women," Josiah said. "More specifically, lovely women."

Anna opened her mouth, then shut it. Her face had to be bright scarlet.

"I don't mean to embarrass you," Josiah said. "I am still mourning my wife and child, but being around you has made me feel . . . a happiness I hadn't expected to ever feel again."

Anna couldn't look away from his earnest gaze, and she wondered if she was truly hearing him right. She hadn't expected him to ever think such a thing, let alone say such a thing to her. And she hadn't expected to feel nervous around him as she did now.

"With the tragedies I've endured, I don't know if I'll ever be as happy as I used to be," he said, "but I look at your family and others around the village and see that they are living full lives despite their own personal challenges. I wanted to tell you thank you, but in truth, I don't know if I could ever thank you enough."

"There is no need," Anna said. "And I am not expecting anything. You work with my father and you've become a friend to Michael."

He nodded. "And a friend to you too, I hope."

"Yes," Anna said quickly. "I'm . . . glad you're doing better. I hope you will feel settled in our village."

"I'm glad I moved here." Josiah rubbed the back of his neck. "Despite my losses, I have been greatly blessed."

"Was it hard to be in the room with widow Tamar?" Anna asked, unable to control her curiosity. "I mean, I don't want to intrude, but I thought it might be more difficult for you because of your recent losses."

Josiah lowered his hand. "When the healer lit the incense, it brought back more than memories. It brought back how helpless I'd been. Have you ever felt that way? That nothing you can do will help?"

"When my mother died, I remember wanting to comfort my father," Anna said. "I was grieving her loss, but I saw a greater and deeper loss in my father. Perhaps I was too young to fully feel the impact as he did or to understand the finality of death. But I wanted to help my father so much. I'd climb onto his lap and hug him, and he'd tell me that was all he needed."

"I can imagine that a man's children would be great comfort after the loss of his wife," Josiah said in a soft voice.

"My father has often said he's honored to have his children so that my mother can live on through us," she said. "I know that you have been left a lone man." Standing by him at the edge of the garden while the hot wind stirred at their clothing made him seem even more forlorn. She had spent enough time here already. "I can come collect the basket later." She turned to leave.

Josiah followed as she walked around the house. "I'm happy to deliver it," he said.

She reached the gate, and Josiah swung it open for her. "All right," she said.

As she walked away, she felt Josiah's gaze on her. What had he meant by his soliloquy? That he was considering marriage again? A family? With her cousin Shoshana speaking for Levi, in a sense, Anna knew the only other man she'd be interested in was Josiah—who was not ready for marriage. She was already past the age of a typical betrothal, and if she married, where would that leave her father and brother?

CHAPTER
THIRTEEN

THE SPRING FESTIVAL WAS TONIGHT, and Josiah should have expected Benjamin to stop him after synagogue classes.

"Would you like to accompany my family to the festival?" Benjamin asked, stepping in front of Josiah before he could exit the building. "My daughters can regale you with all the activities to look forward to."

Josiah had been regaled enough. He'd spent the last Sabbath meal with Benjamin's family, and Rachel had asked him plenty of questions about his garden—something she hadn't been interested in before. Josiah could only assume that Anna had told her cousins about his various mishaps. He couldn't really blame her; it made an entertaining story. But it also made him think of Anna and how he'd rather have Sabbath supper at her home each week. She was a better cook, and the company was less stifling.

At least Shoshana's interest in him had cooled off—not that he was flattering himself, but the attention from both sisters had been overwhelming.

Now Josiah felt trapped. "What time are you leaving?" He thought fast for an excuse—a valid excuse. "I told Phanuel I would help set up some things." He had offered, but Phanuel hadn't said anything since the initial offer. Josiah planned on going early and pitching in wherever he could. He was determined to be a part of the community and not always the one accepting handouts.

"Ah," Benjamin said with a chuckle. "I hope you're handy with a knife and can deal with blisters from tying ropes. We will meet you there, my friend. Be sure to compliment my daughters on their outfits. They've spent weeks on them."

Josiah opened his mouth to reply, unsure of how to respond, but just then, Benjamin saw someone else he wanted to talk to. He bade Josiah farewell and hurried off.

For a few moments, Josiah stood in the shaded entryway of the synagogue. The flowering pomegranate tree nearby scented the air with sweetness, yet the excitement Josiah had felt at the prospect of going to the festival had suddenly waned. He suspected that Benjamin would be watching him all night—watching his interactions with his daughters—perhaps warning others off.

Josiah didn't want to think that he was being guided into taking a specific course of action. If there was a woman in the village whom he was interested in, it was Anna. He could admit that to himself, yet when he nearly confessed his interest in her—as benign as the confession had been—she hadn't returned the expression. He didn't know what he'd expected, but it wasn't her rushing off as soon as she could.

He'd seen her a handful of times since that day she'd helped him kill the beetles in his garden. He'd returned the basket; he'd spent time with her father; he'd even gone fishing again with Michael. But there was a new distance between Anna and himself that hadn't been there before. He wished he could go back to the day in the garden and perhaps just be friendly and not talk about happiness, trials, or losses.

Josiah returned home and changed into his best robe, which probably needed some repair, but he was bent on getting to the main square in time to help Phanuel.

When he arrived, the village men were busy setting up tables, so he pitched in as he greeted those he already knew. By the time he finished with that task, the sun had set, so he also helped light and set up torches. Then the women and children started to arrive, bringing food to place on the tables.

"I've been practicing my knife throwing," Michael said, coming up to Josiah. "Will you be my partner?"

"Ah, I'm not going to be a very good partner," Josiah said.

Michael's face fell. "Father said you could be my partner."

"What I mean is that I haven't been practicing knife throwing," Josiah continued. "I don't want to throw poorly and make you lose."

Michael scrunched his face as he peered up at Josiah. "When did you last practice?"

Never, if Josiah were to own the truth. He used his knife for utility things, not sport. "It's been a long time. Perhaps David is better than I?"

"He's throwing with his father," Michael said. "And my father said he's too old."

Josiah wanted to laugh at the soberness of Michael's expression, but he knew it would only hurt the boy's feelings. "All right, I'll be your partner," Josiah said. "I only wish I knew how to throw better."

Michael grinned and grabbed his arm. "Come with me, and I'll show you how to throw. It's easy—well, it's easy for me."

Josiah chuckled as he allowed Michael to pull him toward a row of grain sacks set up for the knife-throwing game. Each sack was stained with different lines, and Josiah assumed it was how they counted points. The contest hadn't started yet, and a couple of men were practicing with their own knives.

"Here," Michael said, taking out a small knife and tossing it toward a target. The blade hit near the right edge. He shook his head in disgust. "I need to warm up."

Josiah nodded and pulled out his own knife. It had been his grandfather's, and while the blade might have seen plenty of years, it was still a decent knife. He wasn't sure how it would do in a throwing contest though. He took a moment to aim, then threw it toward the target. The blade sank into the grain sack just below Michael's.

"You held it wrong," Michael declared. "You could probably do better if you threw it right."

Josiah smiled. "How should I hold the knife, then?"

Michael leaned close and whispered, "By the blade. My father says it's riskier, but your aim will be more accurate."

Josiah looked about him and didn't see any of the other men who were practicing grasping the blade of their knives. He shrugged and went with Michael to retrieve his knife from the target.

"Watch me," Michael said. "Bring it above your shoulder like this, then throw."

Josiah watched the boy throw. Michael hit closer to the center of the target, but the blade was still out of range of earning any points.

"You try it," Michael said after he retrieved his knife.

Josiah grasped the blade, careful not to hold it too tightly, then aimed and threw. The knife hit right in the center of the grain sack.

One of the men on the other targets released a whistle. Michael stared ahead, his mouth open.

"Luck?" Josiah suggested.

Michael ran toward the target, pried out the knife, then handed it back to Josiah. "Throw it again."

Josiah did, following Michael's earlier instructions. The knife hit true again.

Michael let out a yelp and jumped up and down. "We're going to beat everyone tonight!" He ran and grabbed Josiah's knife, then handed it over again. "Don't throw anymore. We don't want the others to see how good you are."

Josiah nodded, but his mind was reeling. He'd never been in a knife-throwing competition before, so he was interested in how the other men threw their knives. Had he merely been lucky with his throws? Would he be poorer at a greater distance? He'd never had to hunt or go into battle, so he wasn't familiar with most weapons.

The village square had filled up with people in the short time Josiah had been with Michael. Platters of food and baskets of breads and cakes overfilled the tables, and a group of musicians were playing a lively tune. The torchlights brightened the square, casting an orange glow across the many faces in the crowd. Women clustered together, talking, and children ran about in high spirits. Men ate and talked and laughed.

Josiah's attention was drawn to where Anna and her cousins stood together. The women were dressed in fine clothing. Anna's was white and her outer robe a deep blue, with white embroidery along the edges. Her white mantle was also embroidered, and it sat loosely atop her head, covering only half of her dark hair. Shoshana and Rachel were equally adorned, but neither of them matched up to Anna. At least not in Josiah's eyes.

He tore his gaze away, knowing it was impolite to stare. Someone was sure to notice—most likely one of the fathers. He had to put Anna out of his mind. She was of marriageable age, certainly, but looking at her made him feel disloyal to his wife. Yes, he knew Bilhah was gone, but his feelings for her hadn't changed. Couldn't change. He'd left his former home to escape the pressure of another marriage, and yet he was unable to take his eyes off the one woman in the village who had been his friend.

He walked to the food tables, greeting a few people along the way. Michael was off with one of his friends.

"Michael said you have a surprise for us," Phanuel said, coming up to Josiah and clapping him on the shoulder. "What is it?"

Josiah was momentarily stumped. Then he realized Michael must have talked about the knife throwing. "You'll have to wait to see what it is."

Phanuel grinned. "That's what Michael said." He glanced around at the crowd. "Have you seen Anna? I must tell her that her breads were the first to go."

"I saw her awhile ago," he said. It didn't take him long to spot her again since the torches seemed to throw their glowing light in her direction. "She's by the dancers."

Anna stood apart from a group of women who were dancing. It appeared that Rachel and Shoshana were dancing as well.

"There she is," Phanuel said. "Come with me to speak to her. Michael is looking for her since he doesn't want her to miss watching him in the competition."

Josiah couldn't avoid looking at her now. He also remembered Benjamin's insistence that Josiah compliment his daughters tonight.

The women turned when Phanuel joined Anna, and all eyes went to Josiah for a moment.

Josiah greeted the women and added, "You all look very well and festive tonight." He hoped the attention would suffice because he'd just now determined to return home after the knife-throwing competition. It wouldn't be polite to stare at Anna all night.

Anna didn't seem particularly impressed with his compliment, yet Rachel gave him a broad smile, as if he'd spoken the most brilliant words. Shoshana's gaze kept straying from the group.

"Michael wants to be sure that his sister watches the knife competition," Phanuel said.

"Of course I will come," Anna said.

"He has high hopes of winning with his new partner," Phanuel added with a chuckle.

"Oh?" Anna said with a small smile of her own as she peered up at Josiah. Her lashes were dark and her eyes even darker against the torch-lit night. Her white embroidered mantle made a stark contrast to her dark hair and honey-colored skin.

"I hope I can make Michael proud," Josiah said beneath her scrutiny. His heart was drumming in his chest, and he needed to find something else to look at, or he would become a staring fool.

"I should also let you know I've invited Levi over for supper tomorrow night," Phanuel continued.

Anna snapped her gaze to her father's, and Josiah sensed that she was about to argue but changed her mind since she was in public. Perhaps he was reading her wrong. Nevertheless, he wondered how often Levi came for supper. And what did Levi think of Anna? Or more importantly, what did she think of Levi?

Instead of arguing with her father, she nodded, then her gaze slid to Josiah. Something passed between them that Josiah couldn't quite explain, but then it was gone.

"Oh, it looks like the knife-throwing contest is about to start," she said.

Josiah turned to see that a crowd had gathered around the area reserved for the contest, so he hurried over to where Michael was waiting for him apart from the crowd.

Michael grinned when he saw Josiah. "We will be fifth to go—and we'll surprise everyone!" He looked past Josiah. "Oh good, my father and Anna are here."

Josiah looked toward the crowd. Anna stood arm-in-arm with Shoshana, their heads bent toward each other as they discussed something. Rachel waved at him. Phanuel grinned.

Josiah turned back to Michael. "How many throws do we get?"

"Each person gets three, then they total up each team's points," Michael explained.

Josiah and Michael watched the teams of men, with some boys mixed in, as they took their turns. A couple of the throwers hit the center of the targets but only once apiece.

When it came time for Michael and Josiah, Michael said he wanted to throw first. He was handed three knives, and taking the blade in his hand, he tossed the first one. It hit the edge of the grain sack, and Michael groaned, along with the rest of the crowd.

"Just forget the crowd," Josiah told him.

Michael nodded and picked up the second knife. He threw, and this time, the knife landed nearly on the first line of the stain mark.

"Much better," Josiah said. "Now hit the center with this throw."

Michael bit his lip as he picked up the third knife. He closed his eyes for a moment, then opened them and tossed the knife.

It struck nearly at the center of the target. Those around them cheered, and Josiah heard Phanuel cheering above the rest. Michael jumped up and down, then threw his arms around Josiah's waist. Josiah laughed and hugged the boy back.

"Now you just need to hit the center with two of your throws, and we'll win," Michael told Josiah.

If Michael's expression wasn't so hopeful, Josiah might have discouraged him. He picked up the first knife presented to him. Following Michael's previous advice, Josiah grasped the knife by the blade, aimed, and threw. Dead center. The crowd cheered, even though he knew most of them didn't even know him.

Michael grinned. "Again!"

Josiah threw the second knife. Again, it hit dead center.

The crowd cheered again, but instead of it making Josiah feel more confident, he felt more pressure.

"Forget the crowd," Michael said, and Josiah had to smile at that.

Josiah picked up the third knife, aimed, and threw. He didn't realize that he was holding his breath until the air whooshed out of him when the knife hit dead center for the third time.

"You did it!" Michael said, hugging him again.

Josiah could hardly believe it himself. Everyone was cheering, and several people moved close and clapped Josiah on the back, congratulating him.

Phanuel came up to congratulate them, and Anna hugged her brother.

"What do we win?" Josiah asked Michael.

The boy grinned. "A new knife!"

Josiah laughed. "I should have guessed." His gaze connected with Anna's while he was still smiling, and she smiled back. Shoshana and Rachel were with her, and they were all looking at him expectantly.

"You are a skilled man," Anna told him. "And you'll forever be Michael's partner, it seems."

"I've been replaced," Phanuel said, ruffling his son's hair.

"I owe it all to Michael." Josiah glanced at Anna again, even though he tried not to. "He showed me the correct way to throw."

Everyone laughed, and Josiah laughed along with them. He hadn't enjoyed himself this much in a long time, or perhaps ever.

"It seems our new scribe can do many things," Rachel said, moving closer to him and smiling.

Her smile was sweet, but it made Josiah uncomfortable. Perhaps more so because Anna was standing in the group as well.

"What other contests will you be competing in tonight?" Rachel asked.

"This is the only one," he told her. He could feel Anna's gaze on him, and he wished he could be talking to her instead.

"Here is the winning prize," a man said, coming up to them. He held out a knife with a carved wooden handle and a goatskin sheath for the blade.

Josiah took the knife and admired the workmanship, then he handed it to Michael.

"For me?" Michael asked, taking the knife.

"For you," Josiah confirmed.

The man then presented an identical knife to Josiah.

Michael grinned as he slid the knife in and out of the sheath, admiring the blade and the handle. Phanuel took a turn examining the knife, then handed it back to his son.

"Oh, there's Martha," Shoshana said, tugging on her sister's arm. "Let's see if she's brought her baby. Come with us, Anna."

"I'll come in a moment," Anna said, slinging her arm around her brother. "I need to find my brother a treat."

The two cousins left, but Michael squirmed out from beneath Anna's arm. "David and I are doing the honey-cake-eating contest, so I can't eat anything beforehand. There's David now. I'm going to show him my new knife."

Michael left, and Phanuel began speaking to another man nearby, leaving Josiah alone with Anna. At least as alone as they could be at a crowded festival. The musicians struck up a new tune, and many people formed dancing lines. The festival was in full swing.

Josiah stepped closer to Anna so he could speak to her privately. "Does Levi come to your home often for supper?" he asked in a low voice.

She lifted her eyebrows as she looked at him. "What do you mean by 'often'?"

He didn't know whether she was teasing him, but her eyes were bright, her smile soft. His breathing felt stilted, and he knew if he stood here much longer, he might really make a fool of himself. Perhaps it was too late for that. "More often than I?"

Anna's mouth turned up at the corners. "I've known Levi all my life, and he and my father are close."

Josiah nodded, feeling numb. What did that mean exactly? "You are good friends, then."

"We are good friends," she confirmed. "Before he comes to supper, though, I must explain to my father that there's another woman who is interested in Levi in the way that my father hopes I'll be interested in him."

Josiah let her words settle. "You're *not* interested in him?"

"I am not."

The words seemed to put warmth and air back into Josiah's body. But before he could say anything more, someone tapped him on the shoulder. Josiah turned to see Levi, and the man didn't look happy.

"I need to speak with you," Levi said, his gaze moving from Josiah to Anna, then back again.

CHAPTER FOURTEEN

ANNA WATCHED LEVI LEAD JOSIAH away. She had no idea what he might want with Josiah, but the look on Levi's face hadn't been pleasant. She weaved through the crowd, following after the men. For some reason, she felt protective of Josiah. Perhaps it was because he was a newcomer to the village and he'd become a friend of her family. Or perhaps it was because Levi might seem a gentle man, but in truth, he was part of the village brigade that practiced warfare drills several times a week.

But she couldn't think of what Levi might want with Josiah, especially after seeing him win the knife-throwing contest. Her stomach knotted at the thought of Josiah being a part of Levi's group—she knew Levi, being a shepherd, was a lot more familiar with the land and the dangers out there.

Levi and Josiah had left the main crowd and were talking near a group of palm trees. Anna didn't want to interfere with their conversation, so she paused in her step, remaining hidden on the other side of the trees.

Levi's voice carried clearly to her as he said, "We are meeting tonight to assign the next month's patrol."

"I will be there," Josiah responded.

Anna's heart sank as she watched the men shake hands. She was about to return to the festival when Levi said, "Also, I have a message from Benjamin."

Anna stilled and held her breath. What more could Levi ask of Josiah?

"He says that it's not good for a widowed man to spend time with the women of our village," Levi said. "Benjamin says that there is an understanding between you and one of his daughters."

"There is no understanding—" Josiah began, but Levi raised his hand to stop him from continuing.

"I don't need to know any particulars," Levi said. "I am merely passing along the message that Benjamin is concerned, and he will not hesitate to invite you to leave if you mistreat his—"

"I have not mistreated anyone," Josiah cut in. "Benjamin has welcomed me with generosity, but that doesn't mean that I, in turn, will marry one of his daughters. I have not made any promises of doing so. I have simply been a polite neighbor."

The vehemence in his voice echoed Anna's emotions. How dare Benjamin force his way into Josiah's life and decisions?

Levi looked taken aback. "This is not what Benjamin has told me."

Josiah folded his arms. "I have always been a man of my word. I swear on my life."

"All right, then," Levi said, although his tone sounded distrustful. "Tonight, you can prove your loyalty to our village by joining the brigade. We'll not have a man with your skill, scribe or not, sit at home while others are defending his life."

"Are things so bad here?" Josiah asked.

"We've heard rumors the past two days that there have been a few skirmishes in Jerusalem," Levi said. "We never dismiss such rumors. If thieves are driven out of the main city, they always end up in one of the smaller villages, seeking refuge."

"I will be at the meeting tonight," Josiah said.

Levi nodded, then turned away and headed back to the festival.

Anna watched Levi leave, then she looked over at Josiah. He'd turned away too, but it appeared he was heading home and not walking back to the festival. He walked quickly, a purpose to his step, and Anna felt a wave of compassion come over her. Here was a lone man who was trying to start a new life, yet he faced challenges at every turn.

Without thinking about what she might be doing, she hurried after him. When she was within earshot, she called out to him as softly as possible so as not to startle him. It was much darker out here on the road, away from the torches lighting the festival.

He stopped immediately and turned. "Anna?"

He was surprised; well, she was surprised at herself too.

When she reached his side, she said, "I heard some of your conversation with Levi, even though I didn't mean to eavesdrop."

It was too dark to make out Josiah's full expression, but his eyes were on her.

"You happened to overhear the conversation we had in the privacy of a group of trees, away from the festival?"

She exhaled. Was he upset? "When you put it that way, I guess I did have to mean to eavesdrop."

Josiah shook his head, and she still couldn't read his expression. "I seem to have no privacy in this village," he said in a low voice. "If you overhead what Levi said, you know that Benjamin is making quite the case for my betrothal to one of his daughters."

"I did hear that," Anna said. "I suppose it's the nature of things in every village."

"That's what I've found out."

When he went silent, Anna said, "Will you speak with Benjamin to correct him?"

"I have tried to do that already," Josiah said. "It seems the man does not hear my words. He sees only what he wants to see."

The silence extended between them. "What will you do?" Anna finally asked.

"I will speak with your father," Josiah said.

"Oh." Anna was surprised, but perhaps she shouldn't have been. Her father was a good friend to Josiah and would be able to help him. "I hope my father can help you. I have my own matters to discuss with him."

Josiah stepped closer. "Does it have to do with Levi?"

"Yes," Anna said and took a deep breath. She didn't want to betray Shoshana's confidence, but confessing to Josiah felt like the right thing to do. "My cousin Shoshana is in love with Levi."

Josiah didn't say anything for a moment. "Are you in love with Levi too?"

Anna wanted to laugh. First, because he would suggest such a thing. Second, because he seemed so . . . interested in the situation. "Although Levi would make any woman a fine husband, I cannot marry a man my cousin and best friend is in love with. I need to tell my father that I can never marry Levi, no matter what Levi's desires are. I don't know what will happen with Shoshana, but I could never be the one to break her heart."

Josiah seemed to consider her words. "Life is certainly complicated," he said.

That was all he had to say?

"Life is complicated," she agreed. "I hope my father will understand."

"Do you think he'll force you to marry Levi anyway?"

"No." She knew her father would never force her into marriage. Besides, she was happy taking care of him and her brother even though her own years were passing her by.

"I'm pleased to hear that," Josiah said.

She stared at him, dumbfounded. "You are?"

"I want you to be happy, Anna," Josiah said. "That's become very important to me. Which means that I can't spend time alone with you any longer. I don't want village gossip to hurt you. And I need to somehow make it known to the village that I don't intend to marry either of Benjamin's daughters, now or ever."

Anna let the information sink in. She was happy on one hand . . . and on the other . . . "Will you ever marry again, Josiah?"

When he didn't answer for a moment, she worried that she'd crossed the line yet again. She folded her arms against the cool breeze that had kicked up. "I understand if you don't. My father couldn't bring himself to remarry either."

"I am not *against* marrying," Josiah said. "In fact, I have found myself feeling things about a woman that I have not expected to feel again. It has made me feel guilty." Josiah was studying her very closely. "I had determined not to marry again."

The breath left Anna, but she knew this—Josiah had as much as told her.

"Yet . . ." His hand brushed her hand, startling Anna. She was too surprised to move away and even more surprised when Josiah reached for her hand and tugged it free of her folded arms. "I don't want you to take this wrong, but you have changed my mind."

"*Me?*" Anna said breathlessly. "What do you mean?"

"I know I don't want to marry Rachel or Shoshana," Josiah said. "I thought I didn't want to remarry in general. Some days and nights, the pain of my loss is so strong. But since . . . since spending time with you, the ache has dulled and become bearable. It's as if I can see a future again—one that matters. One that might give me a family after all."

He was still holding her hand, and Anna didn't know what to think, what to feel.

"Can you wait for me, Anna?" he asked. "Until I can be a whole man for you?"

She'd heard him, but she couldn't reply. His words were so unexpected, but his hand was like a heated blanket around hers. She had imagined settling for Levi so many times—simple Levi, whom she'd known her entire life. Josiah was complicated. He'd left his village to travel alone. He still grieved over his wife. He'd lost a son. He was a scribe. And he was asking her to *wait* for him?

She knew she wouldn't marry Levi, so what was stopping her from accepting Josiah's proposition? She liked him. She worried about him. She thought about him more than she admitted. She'd even followed him to eavesdrop on his conversations.

"Think about it, Anna," Josiah said. "I know this is sudden and not what you expected. It's sudden for me too. I would like to speak with your father though, if you give me permission."

She felt numb. When he withdrew his hand, the warmth from his body remained with hers. She might have said good-bye, but she wasn't sure. She refolded her arms against the sudden wind as she watched him walk down the road to his home.

Anna didn't know how much time had passed before she returned to the festival. Had she been proposed to? Or was Josiah trying to stall his duties of finding a woman to marry by keeping her in reserve? Was it to stop Benjamin from meddling? Josiah had not told her he loved her, and she hadn't expected him to. What man could love another woman when he was still in love with his dead wife?

Anna had never felt so frustrated and confused in her life. She needed to speak with her father, and she prayed that he would bring clarity to this dilemma and help her. When she found him again, amid all the merriment, she knew tonight wasn't the right time. She would wait until the morrow. Rejoining her cousins Rachel and Shoshana, she acted as if she were enjoying the festival. Yet, her thoughts were still on Josiah.

He had been honest, and she couldn't expect anything more than that. She just didn't know what it would mean for her future.

"Father says I have to walk home with you," Michael said, coming up to her. "He's leaving now. How long are you staying?"

Anna wanted to leave now as well. She looked down at her brother's hopeful eyes. "About another half hour."

"Ah," he said, looking disappointed. "Can I go home when David does?"

"We must listen to Father," she said. "Stay close by."

She turned back to her cousins and was surprised to see that her father had returned to the festival. He stood on the edge of the celebration and was speaking to a handful of men. Even from a distance, Anna could tell he was distressed about something.

"I'll be right back," she told her cousins and hurried over to her father. She reached the group of men just her father was saying, "We must act now, without delay."

The men turned from her father and moved away.

"What's happening?" Anna asked.

Her father's gaze focused on her, his face pale. He drew her close. "Don't panic. But Benjamin's home has been ransacked. I was on my way to our house when his servant stopped me in the road. Only one servant was left home while everyone else came to the festival. Benjamin should be at his house by now to see the damage. I haven't seen it yet, but we need to have his family stay at our home tonight until we know it's safe."

"Was anyone hurt?" Anna asked.

Her father released a breath. "We don't know. We are hoping the only house ransacked was Benjamin's, but there could be more damaged places. We suspect it's the band of raiders that was run out of Jerusalem. Please fetch Michael and your cousins. I will start spreading the word and giving instructions." He looked past Anna, searching the crowd. The music and dancing had already stopped. The men that her father had informed were moving through the crowd, sharing the news, and many people were starting to leave.

"Where's Josiah?" her father asked.

"He left about half an hour ago," Anna said, feeling her stomach twist. "Do you think he's all right?"

"I'll find him" he said. "Stay with your cousins and brother. Don't let anyone go out on their own tonight."

Anna nodded, her heart hammering as she thought of a band of thieves roaming their village in the middle of the night. No one would be safe. She hurried to Michael and grabbed his arm. "We must get home."

This time, he didn't argue. "Did the raiders break into our house?" Michael asked, his eyes rounded with fear.

"No," Anna said, when, in truth, she didn't know. When she spotted her cousins, she hurried to them, Michael next to her.

"Rachel, Shoshana, where's your mother? You are staying with us tonight."

"She's gathering our baskets from the food table," Shoshana said. "Is your father all right with us staying with you tonight?"

"He suggested it." Anna grasped Michael's hand as the crowd surged around them with everyone trying to locate their relatives. They made their way through the crowd and fetched Shoshana and Rachel's mother.

Each of them helped Anna carry baskets, and they set off toward Anna's home. Rumors had grown, and by the time they reached their house, Anna didn't know what was true and what wasn't. Some said the raiders had already been chased off, others said they'd been captured and were being held, and one man said they'd been killed.

Whatever was going on, Anna was glad when they reached her house. Nothing appeared to be disturbed, at least in the front courtyard. She held her breath as she opened the front door and stepped slowly inside. Everything was the same; nothing had been moved or destroyed. With a sigh of relief, she opened the door all the way and ushered everyone inside.

She and her cousins lit the oil lamps in the front room, then Anna went to prepare her bedchamber for her aunt Hannah. Anna would sleep with her cousins.

They all waited together in the gathering room, speculating on what might be happening.

"The village brigade will chase them out," Michael declared.

This thought wasn't exactly comforting because if the raiders had entered another's home, what else might they be capable of? Anna met Shoshana's worried gaze. Without words, Anna could see that her cousin was thinking of Levi. Michael kept on suggesting possibilities, and Anna knew it helped him to talk things through, but her stomach felt like a knotted rope, and it wouldn't release its grip. Her father wasn't a young man, and neither was Benjamin. She wondered if her father had located Josiah.

Another hour passed, and Michael refused to go to his room to sleep, so he dozed off on one of the cushions, his head on Anna's shoulder. When her shoulder became numb from the pressure, she gently moved him so he was in a more comfortable position. Hannah had retreated to the bedchamber some time ago. Rachel was asleep on the cushions, yet Shoshana was still awake.

"How are you doing?" Anna whispered to her cousin.

Shoshana rubbed her face. "I'm so tired that I don't know if this is all real. But I can't stand the waiting and not knowing what's happening with our men out there."

Anna moved to sit by Shoshana, and they clasped hands. "I feel the same way," Anna said. "Short of leaving you all here and running about the village to find out news, I think the only thing we can do is pray."

Shoshana nodded. "I feel like I've been praying all night, but another prayer won't hurt."

Anna released her cousin's hand and clasped her own hands together. Then, in the silence of the house, she whispered a prayer, asking God to protect the families of their village and to protect the men seeking out the raiders. "Bring the raiders to justice, O Lord," Anna prayed. When she finished, she and Shoshana sat in silence for a while.

A knock sounded at the door, startling both of them. Rachel stirred awake, and Anna climbed to her feet. She unlocked the door and opened it to find Levi standing at the threshold. "Is Benjamin's family here?" he asked.

"Yes." Anna opened the door wider. "Come in. Shoshana and Rachel are awake."

Once Levi stepped into the gathering room, where the oil lamps cast their glow, Anna could see that he was dirty and bruised.

Shoshana gasped. "What happened?" she asked, coming forward.

Levi looked down at himself as if he hadn't known anything was wrong. "I'm all right," he said, looking directly at Shoshana. "Your father's been injured. Phanuel is with him now."

Shoshana and Rachel gasped, and Anna said, "What happened? Will he be all right?"

"He has a knife wound," Levi said. "But the healer will be there soon. Phanuel sent me to notify you."

"We must go to him," Shoshana said, looking about wildly. "Anna, we must help my father."

Anna grasped her hand.

"We must wake Mother," Rachel said. "If Father doesn't get better . . ."

"You're right." Shoshana covered her mouth, and tears started.

Rachel hurried from the room to fetch her mother.

Anna knew everyone was in shock; she couldn't quite believe it herself.

"What's going on?" Michael had awakened, and the panic in his eyes was plain.

"Benjamin has been injured," Anna said.

Michael was on his feet. "Did he fight the raiders? Did he catch them?"

Shoshana cried openly, and before Anna could comfort her, Levi had pulled her into an embrace. She cried against his chest as Hannah and Rachel came into the room. Hannah's face was stony, as if she were holding back all emotion at the distressing news.

"We will all come," Anna said, patting Shoshana's shoulder.

Shoshana drew away from Levi and wiped at her face, then nodded.

Anna opened the door, and within moments, they set off toward Benjamin's home.

CHAPTER
FIFTEEN

JOSIAH TURNED AT THE SOUND of footsteps. "Oh, it's you," he whispered, relieved to recognize Levi's form in the dark.

The man crouched beside Josiah with the rest of the men in their group, hiding behind a stone fence. The night had turned cold, and Josiah hadn't taken time to bring an extra robe, but he barely noticed the temperature. The raiders were hiding out in the shepherd field just beyond the village border.

When Levi had knocked on Josiah's door earlier that night and told him what had happened to Benjamin's home, Josiah hadn't hesitated to help. Ironically, he now had two knives, his old one and the one he'd been awarded in the festival. The two men had joined the others, including Benjamin and Phanuel, as they'd scoured Benjamin's property looking for anything the thieves had left behind.

They'd followed a trampled trail through the field behind Benjamin's homestead and come across the remains of a campfire. There, a man had run out of the trees, knife in hand, determined to attack. Benjamin had been closest to the man, and although he'd put up a valiant fight, he'd been struck by the raider's knife. By the time Josiah and the other men had realized what had happened, the raider had gotten away.

They'd chased him, but he'd run like a fox in the near darkness. They'd followed him to the stone fence, which he'd leapt over, and then he'd disappeared into the night. He either went into the hills or crossed the creek or found a cave to hide in. Josiah doubted he was alone, wherever he was.

Now they were waiting for either the clouds to move so they had more light to track the raiders or for the sun to rise.

"How's Benjamin?" Josiah asked as Levi settled next to him.

"The healer has stitched him up and put on a poultice," Levi said. "I fetched his wife and daughters from Phanuel's home. They're with Benjamin now. He's coherent and even drank some of the tea his wife made."

Josiah felt relieved, at least to a point. "What did the healer say?"

"He's positive," Levi said. "But we won't know until tomorrow. As long as there's no fever, he'll probably recover just fine."

"Who else was at Phanuel's?" Josiah asked, hoping he wasn't making his questions too pointed.

"Michael and Anna," Levi said. "They went with Benjamin's family."

Josiah exhaled. "Are there any more reports of break-ins?"

"No," Levi said. "The raiders did a thorough job at Benjamin's though. He's one of the wealthiest men in the village, and it's almost as if they knew where to go."

A shiver traveled through Josiah. No matter the issues he had with Benjamin, Josiah would never wish the man any harm.

Right now, there were five men hiding behind the wall, waiting for any sign of the raiders. They were only half of the village brigade, Levi had said, but the other men were patrolling the village streets to make sure there weren't any other raiders lurking somewhere.

"How are you with a bow and arrow?" Levi asked.

Josiah glanced over at the other men—two of them had bows and arrows. The others carried only knives, like him. "I haven't used one since I was a boy."

"We'll have to remedy that after tonight," Levi said, his voice tight.

If Josiah needed to become an expert with a bow and arrow, he would. He felt a comradeship with these men as they hid out together in the dead of night.

The hours passed, and the closer to dawn it grew, the more restless the men became. Josiah felt it as well. He kept his gaze on the field on the other side of the stone wall, only marginally paying attention to the quiet conversation that sometimes surrounded him. All the men, except for Levi, were married with families. They all wanted to protect their village.

The eastern sky finally lightened, the deep night fading to a lesser gray. The landscape slowly took shape, and Josiah didn't think he'd ever watched the sunrise in this manner. The gray horizon shifted again, turning pale violet, then morphing into blue, with yellow starting to take over as the sun rose.

Josiah trained his gaze once again on the field, scanning every dip and rock and bush. The terrain seemed untouched as the sun's rays started their path along the ground. And then he saw a movement. At first, he thought it was perhaps a hare behind a bush, but then the form that emerged was much larger than a hare.

"Levi," Josiah said. "Look by the left rise."

Levi looked over, and when he stiffened, Josiah knew he hadn't been wrong.

Another form emerged.

Levi alerted the other men, but they'd already seen the forms moving as well. It was time to act. Their plan was to give a good chase to the raiders, and even though they knew they probably wouldn't capture them, Levi hoped it would scare them enough that they'd never return to the village again.

At Levi's signal, all the men climbed over the stone wall and ran. No one made a sound at first; they didn't want to be noticed until it was impossible to conceal their approach.

Josiah didn't have a hard time keeping up with the men since adrenaline was pulsing through him. He knew that after the pursuit, he'd be plenty sore. They sprinted across the field, and now Josiah could see clearly that there were four men who'd been hiding behind the bushes all night, waiting to find their way out by the light of the sun.

When one of the raiders finally heard the approaching runners, he called out to the others, and they started to run.

Good. It was just as Levi had planned.

Josiah's group continued their pursuit, leaping over bushes, kicking up dust, avoiding burrow holes. The raiders charged up a ridge, then over the other side. Josiah didn't slow, and neither did the others. He and Levi were in the lead of their group, the others close behind.

At the top of the ridge, Levi shouted for the others to hold up.

Josiah came to a stop and focused on the scene before him. On the other side of the ridge was a steep descent. It was possible to navigate by foot, but it would be slow going. The raiders had started down it. Once they reached the other side, they would have an advantage to escape.

The men were strong and spry. They might be thin, but they knew how to fight. They had bows slung over their backs, and two of them had knives strapped to their legs. Thankfully, they were retreating instead of turning the pursuit into a battle.

"Let them go," Levi said. "Following them down that descent risks our lives because we'll be trapped. Or one of us could fall. Those men are like goats."

And it was true. They were leaping from rock to rock, grabbing on to protruding plants and roots to prevent their fall down the incline.

Josiah's breath was starting to return to normal. "Do you think they've received our message?"

Levi chuckled. "Yes. We won't be seeing them again."

Just then, the raiders all dropped out of sight, as if they'd plunged off the side of a cliff. But there was no cliff. They'd moved behind some boulders, and the hairs on the back of Josiah's neck rose. Before he could warn the others, an arrow sailed toward them.

"Get down!" Levi yelled as the raiders shot a second arrow.

Everyone dropped to the ground. Next to Josiah, Levi moaned.

Josiah looked over; his new friend had been struck by the second arrow. The shaft stuck out of his thigh, and the wound was bleeding profusely.

"No," Josiah whispered to himself as he scrambled toward Levi.

"Take shelter," Levi told him through gritted teeth. Another volley of arrows rained down, narrowly missing Josiah as he reached Levi.

"Don't touch it," Josiah told Levi when Levi reached for the arrow. "We'll need to cut it out, but for now, we need to tie on a bandage."

With Levi perspiring and moaning, Josiah quickly ripped off a length of cloth from the hem of his tunic. Then he wrapped it around Levi's leg several times, pulling it tight and finally tying it into a knot.

The other men with them positioned themselves behind large rocks and began their own volley of arrows toward the raiders.

"Watch out!" Levi gasped, his voice hoarse.

Josiah dove out of the way, narrowly avoiding an arrow coming right at him. It landed two handspans from Levi. Josiah moved back toward Levi even though his friend tried to wave him off. Josiah pulled him to a sitting position, then wrapped his arms about him from behind and dragged him.

"You're going to get struck," Levi protested.

"I'm not going to watch you become their shooting target," Josiah huffed out. He didn't stop dragging Levi until he had him behind an outcrop of rocks. Then Josiah turned his attention back to the battle.

Three more arrows shot up into the sky. Perhaps one of the raiders had fallen. Josiah looked over at the village men. They had only a couple more arrows among them. It was time for him to make a decision.

"Keep them distracted!" Josiah called out to his men. "Throw rocks, anything."

As the men kicked up their assault by throwing rocks, Josiah crept down the incline, trying to keep out of sight. He took cover behind another outcropping and waited until the next raider rose up to take aim.

Josiah was ready. He threw one of his knives, then ducked out of sight. A solid thump and loud moan told Josiah he'd hit his target. His stomach felt like a stone.

But it wasn't over yet. He waited, trying to calm his breathing so he could hear what the raiders' next move was. More arrows flew, and Josiah rose again, getting into position. There were only two men now. Josiah didn't know what damage he'd done, but it seemed the man he'd struck was possibly hurt enough to no longer be a threat.

Josiah readied his second knife and watched. When one of the raiders rose again, Josiah took aim and waited. The man dove out of sight too fast. Josiah would have to relocate.

Pulse pounding, he looked around but didn't see any other position where he could take shelter. He'd have to go out in the open. So he moved down the incline, no longer protected by the outcropping. When the raiders again took aim, it would be Josiah against two.

There were worse ways to die, he supposed.

When the raiders rose in the next moment, Josiah didn't let himself hesitate. He gripped the knife and threw with all his might. If he missed, the knife striking rock would surely make a mark, but it would mean death for himself.

He didn't miss. The raider cried out and toppled backward.

If only Josiah had another knife, he could throw it at the last raider, who gaped at his companion.

A loud yell from above Josiah caught his attention. The village men were on their feet, scuttling down the ridge, sending rocks and dirt tumbling.

The last raider turned and started to make his own progress down the ridge as if he could outrun the village men. He reached the bottom of the incline, then climbed up the other side. The man made an easy target for a bow and arrow, but Josiah stood watching, not moving, as the man continued his hasty escape.

When the village men reached him, one of them said, "Do you need another knife?"

"No," Josiah said, blowing out a shaky breath. "Someone has to tell the story of how our village defended itself."

"You're right," the village man said. "Well done."

Standing taller, Josiah could see the two lifeless forms of the raiders he'd killed. The third man was several paces away, an arrow in his chest. Three raiders dead. Levi seriously wounded. And who knew how Benjamin was faring at home.

"Let's get Levi some help," Josiah said, trying not to let the sight of the dead men he'd killed bring him to his knees. He turned from the escaping raider, turned from the sight of the dead men lying lifeless in the dirt. His stomach churned, wanting to heave and reject all he'd done and seen. But first, Levi needed help.

CHAPTER
SIXTEEN

ANNA STOOD ARM IN ARM with Shoshana as they waited for the men to come into view. Michael had spotted the village men coming from the field past the border fence, helping an injured Levi, so he had run ahead and told everyone at Benjamin's house, then he'd gone to fetch the healer for the second time.

Michael had said that Levi had been hit by an arrow, but Anna didn't know anything more. What about the other men? What about Josiah?

"I can't stop crying," Shoshana said in a trembling voice as she clung to Anna's arm.

"That's because you've been through a lot." Anna felt like crying herself. But she wanted to support Shoshana. Two men she loved had been injured. Anna had spent the rest of the night at Benjamin's house to help with whatever she could. Neither she nor Shoshana had slept at all. Benjamin had been coherent this morning and had eaten some boiled barley, a promising sign.

And now their worries had been refreshed for Levi and the unknown.

"I see them," Shoshana said, pulling away from Anna.

Anna watched as a group of men came around the bend in the road. Levi was obviously injured, one leg wrapped in a bandage, and two men were helping him walk on his good leg. His face was twisted in pain.

As they drew closer, Anna realized one of the men supporting Levi was Josiah. He looked like he'd been in some sort of fierce battle. From his torn clothing to his scraped and bruised skin, he looked exhausted. The other village men didn't look much better.

"What happened to them all?" Anna asked, mostly to herself.

Shoshana started walking toward them, then she was running. She reached Levi, whose face was so pale that Anna could only guess at the discomfort he was enduring. Shoshana asked questions of the other men, but no one seemed to be able to put what had happened into coherent words.

Anna's gaze met Josiah's, and she saw the hurt there—not only physical but something else too.

Just then, Levi's other leg gave out. Josiah acted swiftly to stop him from falling, and the others helped. They started to carry Levi, and the strain on their faces and arms told Anna they wouldn't be able to support Levi for long.

Shoshana began to cry, and Anna drew her away from the men lest she grew hysterical. "Come, let's prepare a bed for Levi," Anna said.

Shoshana nodded, and they hurried along the road in front of the procession. When they reached Benjamin's house, they set to work quickly. Benjamin had been moved into his bedchamber, and his wife stayed with him to watch over him. By the time the men had brought Levi in, there was a place to lay him down.

As the other men came into the house, Josiah took charge and told the men, "Go home to your families, and let them know you're safe. We'll have the healer help Levi."

The men filed out of the house, and Josiah shut the door, then returned to where Levi was lying on the mat.

Anna and Shoshana were already in the process of cleaning Levi. When they finished washing away the blood and dirt as best as they could without undressing him, Anna sat back while Shoshana was able to persuade Levi to lift his head and take a sip of tea.

Anna looked over at Josiah, who stood, watching them. His gaze was hooded as if he were trying to conceal his thoughts and emotions.

Rising, Anna crossed to Josiah. "Are you all right? Why don't you sit while we wait?"

Josiah didn't have time to respond because just then, the healer arrived, along with Michael. Phanuel had also heard the news and had returned to join everyone at Benjamin's house. It looked as if he hadn't slept either.

The healer's face was grim when he examined Levi. "We need to get this arrow out as soon as possible," he said, looking up at Josiah. "Did you tie on the tourniquet?"

"Yes," Josiah said.

"That probably saved him from bleeding to death."

Josiah nodded, and no one in the room dared to speak. The healer looked from Josiah to Phanuel. "I need two of you to hold him down. He won't like this."

Josiah and Phanuel knelt on either side of Levi and helped hold him down as the healer worked to get the arrow out. Levi stayed alert during the whole thing, but he made a valiant effort not to cry out.

Shoshana gripped Anna's hand as they stood in the entrance of the cooking room, wanting to stay out of the way. When the procedure was over, the healer gave them instructions on how to care for the wound. "He shouldn't be moved for two or three days," the healer said.

"He can remain in our home," Shoshana was quick to reply.

Eventually, when color had returned to Levi's face, Anna felt like she could breathe easier. Color returned to Shoshana's face as well.

Phanuel left with the healer to go check on the other men who'd been in the group. After they left, Levi spoke his first coherent words since he'd arrived. "Thank you, Josiah," he said, his voice hoarse. "You saved our lives."

"I didn't do anything you wouldn't have done," Josiah said.

Levi shook his head. "We'll never know, but you were fearless."

Josiah released a shaky laugh. "I wouldn't exactly say that."

"You should get some rest," Levi continued. "You look terrible."

Josiah's smile was more genuine this time. "You should sleep too."

The edges of Levi's mouth curved. "I'm nearly there."

After Levi shut his eyes, Shoshana turned to Josiah. "Thank you for bringing him back. I don't know all that happened, but our prayers have been answered."

Josiah nodded. "I'll be back to check on him in a few hours. How's your father doing?"

"Much better," Shoshana said.

Josiah glanced at Anna as if he wanted to say something, but he changed his mind and didn't speak. He crossed the room and went to the door, then left.

Anna waited a moment, then decided to follow. She had to ask what had happened. She had to find out if he'd be all right. Did he have food at home?

Josiah had reached the gate by the time Anna came out of the house. He paused when he heard her, and she hurried across the courtyard.

"I'll be all right," he said without meeting her gaze.

She didn't say anything, just waited for him to open the gate. When he did, he motioned for her to go ahead of him. They walked a ways down the road. Everything was quiet this morning; it seemed the villagers were keeping to themselves and getting much-needed rest. The sun was already warm, and the day promised to be hot.

Anna stole a couple of glances at Josiah, and he seemed lost in his own thoughts.

"You are uninjured?" Anna finally said, breaking the silence.

He slowed his step as if he had to think about her question. "I'll have a few bruises."

Silence again. They walked the rest of the way to his house. He opened the gate and held it. Anna's heart leapt—maybe he would talk to her about the incident. She hoped that talking about it would help diminish the pain she could see in his eyes.

He didn't lead her into his house; even in his distress, he knew what was proper. They walked around the house to where his fledging garden was. The plants looked young and strong, but now wasn't the time to comment on it.

He crossed to the goat pen and scratched the head of his lone goat.

The palm tree near the pen provided sparse shade, and Anna took advantage of it. "What happened out there?" she asked in a quiet voice. "Did the raiders flee after they injured Levi?"

Josiah stepped back from the goat. He looked at her, then looked away. It took him another long moment to speak. "We chased them across the field toward the hills. When we thought we'd chased them off for good, they turned on us." He closed his eyes and rubbed his forehead. "They had bows and arrows, and Levi got hit."

Anna folded her arms, feeling chilled even though the heat of the morning should have kept her warm. She had assumed what Josiah was telling her. But what *wasn't* he telling her? She waited for him to continue.

When he finally did, his voice was low, almost hoarse. "After Levi was hit, I couldn't just let them keep shooting arrows at us." He paused as if he were second-guessing telling her anything more. "I couldn't let them hurt anyone else . . . I couldn't . . ." His voice broke, and he turned away.

Anna blinked back her own tears. She still didn't know what had happened, but the tremor in Josiah's voice tore at her heart. She touched his arm, then removed her hand quickly, wishing there were something she could do. "You did what was right. Levi will be fine. The other men were only bruised. You ran the raiders out of the village. Everyone is grateful."

Josiah turned and looked at her, his eyes rimmed with red. "You don't understand, Anna," he said in a stilted voice. "I killed two men. I used both my knives." He shuddered. "The third man was killed by an arrow. The fourth man escaped."

Anna couldn't move, couldn't breathe. Josiah's gaze seemed to be imploring her for answers. Life could be brutal, and sometimes men had to defend their homes in violent ways. She could see the mixture of regret and anger in his expression.

"I killed two men," he whispered.

Anna couldn't think of anything to do but to grasp his hand. He didn't move for a moment, then he wrapped his fingers around hers. She felt his pulse pounding and his hand trembling, with sorrow, with anger, with disbelief . . . she didn't know what exactly. But she continued to hold his hand, and it felt right to try to comfort him in this way. "You didn't have a choice," she said. "You were defending your own lives, your neighbors, your property, and our village."

He lowered his head so his face was close to hers. He didn't audibly cry, but by the shaking of his shoulders, Anna knew he was grief-stricken.

"I hate what I did," he said after a moment, his voice still a whisper.

"I know," she whispered back. "Sometimes our choices aren't easy."

After awhile, he seemed to relax. His hold on her wasn't as tight, and he stopped trembling. When he pulled away, he was calmer and more composed.

Anna reluctantly released his hand.

"I'm sorry for burdening you," he said.

"You've never been a burden," she said. The pain in his eyes was still there, but he seemed more serene. "Do you need help cleaning up?"

His face flushed, and Anna realized how her question must have sounded.

"I mean, do you need help with anything?"

"No," he said, clearing his throat. "You're right. I need to clean up, and then I should try to sleep."

Anna nodded. "We're all tired, but you especially." She gave him a hopeful smile and turned to go.

"Anna?" Josiah said, his voice still soft.

She paused and turned.

"Thank you."

Anna nodded and continued around the house. She couldn't get the look of anguish she'd seen on his face out of her mind. She hurried along the road, back home to see if Michael needed anything.

She entered her home to find him waiting.

"Is Levi all right?" Michael asked, worry in his tone. "Father made me come home and told me I had to get some sleep."

"Levi's going to be fine," Anna said. She looked about the cooking room and saw that Michael had eaten all the leftover bread.

She warmed up the barley soup, and as they ate, Michael said, "Did you hear what Josiah did?"

Anna wasn't sure how much her brother knew, so she said, "Let's not spread gossip. Father can tell us what we need to know."

Michael didn't argue, which told Anna he was extremely tired. When he finished his soup, he went into the gathering room and nestled against the cushions. Anna let him nap there, sensing he felt more secure in the fact that he wouldn't miss anything when their father returned home.

She cleaned up the simple meal, keeping the pot of barley soup over the coals so her father might have nourishment when he returned. Then she too reclined on the cushions to await her father's return. She was tired enough to fall asleep immediately, but her mind wouldn't stop turning over what Josiah had told her. She couldn't stop thinking about how he'd looked at her. How he'd trembled with his grief and how much it had affected him to kill those raiders.

A shiver traveled through her, and she hoped he wouldn't ever have to be in that situation again. She hated to see him in so much emotional turmoil, and the haunted look in his eyes felt like a knife twisting in her own chest. She closed her eyes against the images her imagination created and said a silent prayer for everyone involved—Josiah, Benjamin, Levi, and the others.

Anna must have finally fallen asleep, because sometime later, she was awakened when her father came home. Michael continued to sleep, and Anna rose quietly to greet her father. He kissed her on the cheek, then pulled her into a rare embrace.

When he drew away, he cradled her face with both hands. "How are you, Anna?"

Tears burned at his question, catching her off guard. She hadn't meant to cry. Perhaps it was because she felt safe with her father, and he was finally home. "I am well," she said. "I took a nap, and Michael is still sleeping."

Phanuel nodded. "I think I will sleep for a little while too. Benjamin is on the mend. Levi is trying to get up, much to Shoshana's dismay."

Anna found herself smiling. She could only imagine the scene.

Then her father sobered. He lowered his hands and grasped hers. "I visited with Josiah, and he is very upset."

The tears started again. Anna could only nod.

"He told me you know what happened."

She nodded again.

"I'm afraid it might take him some time to work through his emotions," her father continued. "When I had hoped . . ."

"Hoped what?" Anna said when he stopped talking.

"That he would offer for your hand in marriage."

Anna couldn't have been more surprised at the turn in the conversation. Maybe she was asleep and dreaming all of this. "Josiah's grief over his wife is still fresh."

"Yes, he told me," her father said.

"He told you that too?"

"Come," her father said, motioning for her to join him in the cooking room, where they wouldn't have to be so quiet on account of Michael still sleeping.

Once they were sitting around the table, Phanuel said, "When we were in that room with Levi being worked on, I realized I've been quite oblivious to Shoshana's feelings toward Levi. And perhaps his feelings toward her?"

It was a question, and Anna knew the answer. "I believe he cares for her as well."

"Ah," her father said. "Yet Levi is a shepherd, and although he's a fine man, Benjamin would want his daughter to have a more secure life."

Anna nodded at this, but she didn't let her hope falter. She knew her father well enough to see that he was seriously considering options.

"And then . . . the way Josiah has seemed to rely on you and your concern over his well-being . . ." Phanuel rubbed his beard. "I think Josiah cares for you, Anna. More than he expected to care about another woman for a long time. I don't blame him, of course. You are a wonderful young woman."

Anna's mouth went dry. Even if Josiah did care for her, he'd as much as told her he was still a broken man. And now, with the battle against the raiders, he was having an even harder time.

"I don't think Josiah wants to be pushed into anything," she said. "But I am not sorry to lose Levi to Shoshana. They truly care for each other in a much deeper way than I ever cared for Levi."

Her father nodded as if he'd been expecting that reply. "After Josiah told me all his concerns, he told me something else that will interest you."

What now? Anna wondered. What more could happen in a single day?

"He said he doesn't want to wait to marry. He cares for you, and he knows his affection will only grow. Yet this morning, he said he saw the face of death and stood toe to toe with his own mortality. He wants to return to a full life, one without fear, without grief, and he wants you by his side as his wife."

CHAPTER
SEVENTEEN

JOSIAH PICKED UP HIS WIFE's half-embroidered mantle. It had been a reminder to him of a life unfinished. A life gone too soon. He'd been witness to how abruptly a life could end, either at a man's hands or God's. There had been too much death surrounding him, and he felt like he was suffocating because of it.

He brought the mantle to his face and inhaled the faint scent. It no longer smelled of her but of earth and dust. Carefully, he folded it and carried it into his bedchamber. There, in the crate he'd brought most of his things in from his previous home, he set the mantle. It would be protected from light, and perhaps the woven colors would hold fast longer.

But he decided that seeing the mantle every day was renewing his grief time and time again. He would never truly stop grieving Bilhah, but if he were to welcome a new wife into his heart and home, he needed to put more faith into moving forward.

It had been nearly a week since he had spoken to Phanuel about marrying his daughter. They'd had a few conversations since then, and each time, Phanuel had said Anna would be making the decision. Josiah didn't expect anything less from a father like Phanuel—a father who'd taught his daughter to read and write.

In all this time, Josiah hadn't seen Anna. He'd even passed by her home more than once but hadn't caught a glimpse of her. Some good news was that Phanuel had said Benjamin's heart was softening toward Levi—who had become one of the village heroes due to the incident with the raiders. Some folks in the village had praised Josiah as well, but he had kept the harsher details of the incident private.

What did Anna think of him, and was there a reason Phanuel couldn't tell Josiah about his daughter's wishes? Josiah could not keep living in this state of uncertainty, and he felt even worse knowing that he'd asked Anna to wait for him that night at the festival. He knew now that he couldn't expect that of a woman who might want a family of her own sooner rather than later.

He knew he cared for Anna, perhaps even loved her if it weren't for the heavy weight resting on him, and he wanted her to be happy. He'd enjoyed every moment they'd spent together, and he could admit that he found her beautiful and desirable. But he worried that Anna had been put off by him. Her father had been kind enough to him, yet Josiah felt the silence and absence of Anna keenly.

Tonight, he'd determined, he would visit Anna's home and seek audience with her. For better or for worse, at least after tonight he would know what his future might bring.

The sun was halfway hidden on the western horizon when Josiah set off for Anna's home. As he walked through his courtyard, he couldn't help but be pleased by how much better the shabby, small homestead looked. The results of weeks of labor had produced a repaired gate, a sturdy stone wall surrounding the property, a working water fountain, a fledging garden, a well-constructed goat pen, and pruned vines that climbed one side of the stone wall.

He still had plenty of work to do on the inside of the house, but it was cleaned out and ready for new memories to be made. Ironically, he hoped Anna would be a part of those memories when just a month ago, he'd come to this village hoping to hide out from any sort of marital relationship or responsibility. Now

Anna dominated his thoughts during the day and infiltrated his sleep during the night.

This was right. Being with Anna was right. He just hoped she believed the same.

"Josiah," a man said, pulling him out of his thoughts.

He looked ahead on the road and saw Levi coming toward him. Each time Josiah saw his new friend about the village, a rush of gratitude flowed through him at the sight of his returned health.

"How are you?" Levi asked.

"I should be asking how *you* are doing," Josiah said.

The man walked with a limp, but otherwise, he appeared healthy and sturdy. "I am faring well," Levi said. "I've been in the fields today for the first time since my injury. I'll probably suffer some achiness tomorrow, but it's nothing to complain about."

Josiah nodded. "It's good to see you doing so well."

Levi clapped a hand on Josiah's shoulder. "I'll never forget what you did for me and the other men. Our entire village, in fact."

Josiah felt the familiar ache in his chest start up. "I . . . didn't know what else to do."

"You did the only thing you could," Levi said. "You saved our lives."

Josiah let his friend's words settle into his heart and mind. He had spent hours scrubbing away dirt and blood that day, but he could still see it on his skin, if only in his mind. Perhaps in time, he would no longer see the stains.

"Where are you heading?" Levi asked.

"I'm—" Josiah paused. "I'm going to Phanuel's home."

"Ah," Levi said with a grin. "Are you going to try to talk his stubborn daughter into something?"

"How did you know—?" Josiah started when Levi laughed.

"Shoshana has told me a few things," Levi said. "Nothing that I can pass on, but I'm pleased to see you are going to her home tonight."

Josiah was more than curious, but he also wanted to ask something else. "You and Shoshana?"

Levi continued to smile. "You have brought many miracles to this village, Josiah. I have much to thank you for. Because of you, Benjamin has just agreed to have Shoshana become betrothed to me."

Josiah's brows shot up.

"Don't look so surprised," Levi said with another laugh. "Benjamin told me less than an hour ago that he'd be pleased to call the village hero his son-in-law."

"You're a good man, and Benjamin *should* be pleased," Josiah said in a genuine tone.

Levi sobered. "You're a good man too, Josiah. Don't forget that. And know that all you need is a little patience with Anna. Shoshana says she'll come around."

"I hope Shoshana is right," Josiah said, feeling the conviction deep inside and wondering whether he had said too much.

After leaving Levi, Josiah's step was lighter. As he approached Phanuel's home, he was surprised to see Anna on the road, walking from the other direction. She was alone and carried a basket. Josiah could only assume she'd been delivering something to a person in need—such was her habit.

She slowed her step when she saw him, and he wasn't sure if that was a good thing or a bad thing. Was she hesitant to be around him? Was his confession to her father putting her in a position she didn't want to be in?

Josiah continued toward her gate and stopped so she would know he'd meant to come to her house.

"Good evening," Anna said, reaching the gate herself.

He searched her gaze for something more than just a pleasant greeting. "Hello, Anna."

"Is my father expecting you?" she asked, opening the gate and stepping through.

Josiah followed her. "No, I was coming to speak with you."

At this, she stopped and looked up at him. She shifted the basket to her other arm.

"Is that heavy?" Josiah asked. "I can carry it for you."

"No, it's empty," Anna said. "I was taking something to Tamar's daughter's family."

Of course she was. Josiah nodded. "You have a habit of doing nice things for people."

Anna's mouth lifted ever so slightly, and Josiah took it as encouragement.

"You are looking well," she said, then looked away for a moment. When her gaze returned to his, she added, "I was worried about you, but my father gave me some updates."

"Your father has been helpful," he said. "As well as Levi. They have told me the things that you told me. I wanted to thank you for . . . helping me when it was so difficult."

Anna nodded but didn't say anything. It was like they had an unspoken understanding between them, and more words didn't need to be said. She took a few more steps and set the basket on a stool beneath the pomegranate tree.

When she straightened, she faced him again, and he saw the curiosity in her hazel eyes.

He wasn't here to talk about the past; he wanted to talk about the future. He just hoped she would be receptive. "I am sure your father has spoken to you about the entirety of our conversations?" His heart rate went up a notch as her gaze remained on him.

"He has."

He could see she wasn't going to make this easy for him. "Anna, what I said at the festival was the truth of my feelings," he said. "I'm still a broken man."

Anna waited for him to continue.

"I realized something this week though," Josiah continued in a quiet voice. "I will always be a broken man. Whether it's from one life experience or another, we will all continue to have challenges."

Anna's expression softened.

"And I know that you're wholly devoted to caring for your father and your brother," Josiah said. "This is no small thing, and

I've considered your obligations to your family and your desire to continue in your education."

Her brows shot up at this comment.

"Anna," Josiah said, feeling his throat tighten. "I care deeply for you, more than I thought it would be possible to care about another woman after the loss of Bilhah. I was caught off guard, not expecting to have these types of feelings toward a woman again, or at least so soon."

Anna didn't move, didn't blink. But she was listening to every word.

"You and your family have taken care of me since my arrival," he said, "and you have also given me a new sense of why it's so important for families to help and support each other. But most of all, when I look at you, I don't want to say goodbye. When I'm around you, I only want to spend even more time with you."

Anna exhaled. She seemed to be gathering up her courage. "I can't replace your wife, Josiah. I am my own person."

The insecurity in her gaze tore at his heart. He didn't expect her to be anything like Bilhah. "I know," he said. "I want to marry *you*, Anna, because you're Anna. Not because I'm a lonely man in need of a wife."

She tilted her head, a slight smile curving her lips.

"All right, I am a lonely man in need of a wife," Josiah said, feeling a smile tug at his own mouth. "But that is not why I want to marry you."

She exhaled and folded her arms. "I am perfectly happy caring for my family, Josiah. Why should I abandon them and live in your rundown home?"

If she hadn't been smiling, he might have been offended.

"That rundown home is already much better," Josiah said, stepping closer to her. "And you won't be far from your family. They can come for meals every night if they want to."

She gave a short laugh.

"And . . . I think you care for me too," he said, although he uttered it more as a question. "Or perhaps you are kind and generous to every widower in the village?"

Anna took a step back, her eyes fiery. "Certainly not."

"Then . . . you do care for me?"

She seemed to waver—in her decision or in making a confession, Josiah wasn't sure. "I do care for you, Josiah. You are a good man."

Josiah wanted to groan with frustration. But then she stepped closer and said in a quiet voice, "Thank you for the offer of marriage. I will think on it."

Josiah's mouth almost fell open. After all of this, she said she would think about it?

But before he could respond, she turned and hurried into the house, leaving a swath of darkening night between them.

CHAPTER
EIGHTEEN

"Was that Josiah?" Michael asked as Anna entered the house.

"Yes," she barely managed to say. She was out of breath for some reason, probably due to the way her pulse was pounding. Josiah had asked her to marry him. Now, in the present. Not in the future.

"Why did you let him leave?" Michael said, moving toward the door as if he were about to go after him. "David is ill, so maybe Josiah can go fishing with me tomorrow."

Anna moved to block the door. "Don't go out there."

Michael's brows pulled together. "Why not?"

"Because . . . because he asked me to marry him, and I told him I'd think about it."

Her brother's eyes widened, then he let out a whoop. "Josiah will be my brother!" He began to do some sort of a lunging dance, and Anna grasped his upper arm to stop him.

"I haven't given him my answer yet."

Michael shrugged. "Well, I know you're going to say yes, so I'm going to celebrate now."

Anna didn't know whether to laugh or get mad at him. She shook her head and walked through the house. Her father was in the back courtyard with his scrolls. She exited the house, and he looked up as she came outside.

"Are you ready to do some reading?" he asked.

Anna nodded and sat, then pulled a scroll toward her. She started to read, but she couldn't concentrate. The silence between her and her father was comfortable, but her thoughts were tumultuous. She loved the order and peace of her home. The predictability. The chance to raise her brother and to care for her father. If she left, her brother's routine would not be as closely watched. Her father wouldn't have a woman in the home taking care of domestic matters.

Could she really leave them and be a wife?

It wasn't just that Josiah had asked the question; she was now realizing why she was yet unmarried. She'd never given any man encouragement before. She never prodded her father to change her position. Deep inside, she was content with her life. The loss of her mother had taught her to value her father and brother as never before. Their small family was such a close unit, and truthfully, she didn't want anything to change that.

Anna released a breath and rested her head in her hands.

Her father didn't say anything for a moment, although he surely noticed that she was no longer reading. Then he asked, "Do you want to talk about what's troubling you?"

She shrugged, and her father's voice was tender when he next spoke. "I'm assuming this is about Josiah. I know he came over earlier, and I want you to know that your brother and I will be fine. We are only a short distance away, after all. We could still have a meal together on many nights."

"That's what Josiah said," Anna confessed.

Her father took her hand in his and squeezed. "I won't be around forever, and Michael will marry and have his own children someday. What then, Anna? You deserve to have a husband. You deserve to have your own children and your own grandchildren."

Tears stung Anna's eyes at her father's words. "I don't know how other daughters do it."

"They don't have as nice a family as you do, I suppose," her father said.

Anna smiled through her tears.

Her father moved closer and put an arm around her. "I know that change is hard and that the future is unknown to us. Yet Josiah is a good man, and he loves you."

Anna lifted her head. "He hasn't said so."

"He will," her father said. "If that is what makes the difference to you, you can rest assured. I think Josiah is as caught off guard as you are. His experience with the raiders has taught him, and all of us, that putting off the important things in our lives isn't going to make life easier. We need to do what our hearts are telling us to do now, no matter how much we might fear it."

"So he fears marrying me?" Anna said, mostly teasing. Her heart did feel lighter.

"He fears losing you and having his heart broken again." Her father paused. "He knows that marrying you is the right decision though. He knows that he was brought to our village by the Lord because this is the direction his life needed to take. But he is also afraid to believe in good things."

Anna went silent. She was afraid to believe in good things too. Right now, without Josiah, she knew she could be happy. She also knew Josiah was a good man and that she'd fallen in love with him. Still, she was afraid to make that change, take that risk of giving her heart and soul and body over to another person. To bring children into the world who might face illnesses, trials, or premature death.

She leaned her head against her father's shoulder. "Were you nervous to marry Mother?"

Her father chuckled. "I'd been in love with your mother since I first saw her. I suppose that was a blessing because I lost her so early. She wasn't as quick to return my affection, but our families approved the betrothal, and I believe I eventually charmed her into loving me."

Anna laughed at this. She knew her mother had loved her father deeply. He was just being modest. "We were all fortunate to have her."

"Yes," her father whispered. "And she would want her only daughter to seek after happiness and live a life of joy. We know trials will continue to come, but we need to embrace our blessings and show the Lord our gratitude for our lives by living them to the fullest."

Anna nodded; the tears were back. She released another sigh.

"Without thinking of me or your brother, what does your heart tell you?" her father asked.

She wiped at her eyes, then said in a trembling voice, "My heart tells me to marry Josiah."

Her father squeezed her shoulder. "You will make a good wife and find much happiness."

"Oh, Father, I hope you're right." Anna lifted her head and smiled through new tears. "At least Michael will be excited."

"We're all happy for you," her father said with a tender smile. "You deserve everything life can offer. Go and give your answer to Josiah. Don't make the man lose any more sleep."

She took a shuddering breath. "All right." She rose and left the courtyard, walking around the house so she wouldn't encounter Michael. Josiah should be the next one to know, not her younger brother.

The sun had set by now, and the western horizon displayed a splash of violet and blue. She could hardly believe she was about to become betrothed. Women who were betrothed at younger ages would typically have a one-year betrothal period. Anna doubted hers would be that long.

She slowed her steps as she reached Josiah's house. There was a faint glow coming from inside, so she knocked on the front door. When no one answered, she wondered if he'd left an oil lamp burning and was at a neighbor's. She decided to walk around the house to see if, by chance, he was in the back courtyard. She found him there, sitting on a bench, lost in thought.

He turned his head as soon as she approached, and his expression went from surprise to hope, then to wariness all in the same breath.

"Anna," he said, getting to his feet. "Is everything all right?"

"Yes." Her voice shook. "I've come with my answer."

"Already?" His brows furrowed as if he were steeling himself, expecting her to turn down his marriage proposal.

"Already." She tamped down a smile as she stepped closer. "I've spoken with my father . . . and my brother," she added, for it was true. "And I've decided to accept your proposal of marriage."

Josiah stared at her for a moment, but instead of looking pleased, he looked wary. "Is this because your father and brother approve or because you want to marry me?"

She hesitated, wondering how early was too early to fully confess her feelings. "I do want to marry you, Josiah, and it's not because of my father or my brother. But they have certainly been supportive, which is very important to me."

He nodded. "That's important to me as well." There was new hope in his tone.

She took another step toward him and stood close, not touching him. "Yes, I do care for *you*, Josiah. And I most likely love you as well." Her cheeks were warm, and that warmth spread along her neck at her confession.

He studied her for a moment. Then he bent and said close to her ear, "I love you too, Anna. It frightens me how much."

Anna closed her eyes. She could feel his whispered breath brush against her ear and neck, but he still wasn't touching her. Regardless, warmth continued to spread through her body. "I know you're fearful," she whispered back. "But you are also brave."

She sensed his smile, although she didn't see it. Then she felt his lips press against hers so briefly that she almost questioned it. But the tingles racing through her body were real. Fortunately, she and Josiah were out of sight of others, aided by the growing night.

When she opened her eyes, Josiah took her hand in his.

"Thank you for making me a happy man, Anna," he said, his voice still soft.

Peering into his eyes, she saw relief there and even wonder. She felt the same.

"Let's go tell my brother," Anna said, though she was reluctant to terminate their privacy. She knew that being alone with Josiah for too long might tempt her to kiss him as well.

"If you insist."

She didn't need to insist, but she was happy Josiah listened to her and respected her wishes. He led her around the house by her hand, and she reveled in the warmth and strength of his fingers. She looked forward to this man loving her and taking care of her.

When they reached the road, he let go of her hand. Even though it was nearly dark, it wouldn't do to pass by other people while holding hands. The news would spread faster than the time it took Anna to reach her home.

As suspected, her father and brother were both waiting for them. Michael opened the door before Anna could even reach it. He looked like he was ready to burst with excitement, and instead of running to embrace his sister, he embraced Josiah.

Josiah chuckled and squeezed Michael back. Over the top of Michael's head, Josiah met Anna's gaze and smiled. Her heart swelled at the sight, and she was suddenly very pleased that she'd decided to answer him tonight. Because, really, what was the use of putting him off for even one more day?

Her father was grinning inside the house. Josiah and Michael followed Anna in, and the men settled in the gathering room. Anna went to prepare some refreshment while Michael peppered Josiah with questions.

When Anna returned with a tray of sweetened dates and honey cakes, Michael was telling Josiah how being brothers meant that Michael wouldn't have to ask his father for permission for everything.

"Slow down, Michael," Josiah said in a jovial tone. "Your father is still your father. Even at my age, I can't make his decisions for him."

Michael shrugged that off. "When are you getting married?"

Josiah's gaze once again met Anna's as she sat across from him on her own cushion.

"We haven't talked about a date yet," Josiah said.

Michael had an opinion on this too. "I hope it's soon because Father said that when Anna gets married, I'll get to move into her bedchamber."

Anna shook her head while the men laughed.

After the conversation and congratulations with her family, Anna and Josiah left the house and walked to the gate. The rising moon was bright in the full darkness of the sky. Josiah slipped his hand around Anna's, and she smiled up at him.

"Michael seems very excited about our news," she said.

Josiah chuckled and pulled her close, and Anna rested her head against his chest. She couldn't explain how wonderful it felt to have this man's arms around her and to feel the steady beat of his heart against her ear. "I am excited about our news too."

Anna knew nothing was perfect between them and that challenges would be a part of their lives, but she decided to enjoy this moment. She wrapped her arms about his waist, feeling his warmth. "I can hardly believe this is all happening."

Josiah kissed the top of her head, which only made her heart rate speed up. "When should we get married?" he asked.

She smiled. "A year is our village's betrothal custom."

Josiah groaned. "I think we can forgo that tradition. I'm a widower, and every day you grow older," he said in a teasing voice.

"Should I take offense at that?" she asked.

Josiah only pulled her closer. "It's much to my advantage. How soon will be proper enough?"

"At least a month," Anna said.

"Then we'll marry exactly a month from today."

Anna pulled away enough to look up at him in the moonlight. "You are an impatient man."

Josiah lifted a hand to trace a finger along her cheek, sending warmth skittering down her neck. "I am impatient to finally start living the rest of my life."

Then he bent down, and Anna's heart seemed to leap toward him. His second kiss was more determined and sure than his first kiss had been. His lips were warm, searching, yet full of love and promise. Anna kissed him back, knowing she was inexperienced but hoping that Josiah also felt the love she was happy to offer.

"Anna," he whispered, breaking away. "Even a single month will be hard to wait."

She agreed, but she needed the time to prepare. She let her fingers move through the ends of his hair, then she caressed his neck. "The wait will be worth it, I am sure."

His smile was genuine, and when he kissed her in a final farewell, she was grateful that she was at last seeing Josiah open up and be his true self.

CHAPTER
NINETEEN

Present Day

"WE MARRIED ONE MONTH AND one day after I accepted Josiah's proposal," Anna said, smiling through tears. Even though so much time had passed, she still remembered the excitement of her wedding day. It seemed the entire village came to their wedding feast, and the entire day was filled with joy and love. She had never told her story so fully, and in doing so, it had brought all her memories to the surface at once.

She blinked back tears as Julia reached over to grasp her hand. This great-niece had been a blessing in her life in only the few short days they had lived together. The hour was quite late now, and Julia had added more oil to the lamp at one point. But Anna had continued to tell the story of her beloved Josiah. It seemed once she'd started, the entire story had spilled out of her. Many of the memories had faded long ago, but with Julia's eager gaze on Anna, she found herself remembering so many things.

Like the morning she'd said goodbye to Josiah, not knowing it was the last time she'd see him alive.

"Rumors of the destruction by Pompey's army reached our small village quickly," Anna told Julia. "Josiah and the other men wasted no time in preparing their weapons and setting up a border guard."

Anna still remembered the warm summer morning and how Josiah had risen before dawn, unable to sleep. She hadn't slept much the night before either, so she'd joined her husband to watch the sunrise from the courtyard, standing hand in hand. Even though Anna had remained barren, their marriage and family had felt complete. Maybe it was the way Josiah had always made her feel valued and important, so she didn't feel so much of the pain of not being a mother to her own child.

When she saw the tall, gangly form of her sixteen-year-old brother coming down the road to join up with Josiah, Anna keenly felt the weight of what they were about to do.

Michael looked as if he'd been up all night too. He didn't seem tired and worried like Josiah but excited to be part of such an adventure.

Anna kissed and embraced her brother, who'd grown a full head taller than she. Then she turned to Josiah. "Be safe," she whispered and raised up on her toes to kiss his cheek.

Josiah pulled her into his arms and held her tightly for a few moments. Anna hugged him back, wishing she didn't have to let go. But Michael was waiting, probably rolling his eyes at their display of affection. She and Josiah had been married seven years, yet Anna never tired of how it felt to have her husband's strong and comforting arms about her.

"I'll watch over Michael," Josiah said, and Anna knew he would.

If Pompey's soldiers advanced on their village, the men would be in danger, especially those such as Michael who had less experience than the others. It brought Anna comfort knowing that Josiah would watch out for her brother, yet that didn't ease her worry over Josiah's own safety.

Anna's heart tugged as she stood at the gate and watched her husband and brother walk down the dirt road, joining the other men of the village, including Levi, who had married Shoshana and now had three children.

Once Anna's husband and brother were out of sight, she walked to her father's home, where they would wait together for news.

"I didn't know that by nightfall I'd be a widow," Anna told Julia, refocusing her attention on her audience. "If I had known, I wouldn't have let Josiah leave our house in the first place."

Julia's eyes widened with sympathy. "Do you really think you could have prevented him from leaving?"

After a moment's thought, she said, "No. Nor could I have prevented my brother from leaving." She took a deep breath. "Levi was the one who brought Michael back to my father's home and delivered the news of Josiah's death. Michael was unconscious and seriously injured." Even now, in the stillness of the deepening night, Anna remembered the horror of that night. It had been decades since her loss, yet she still felt Josiah's absence keenly. "Although I had only been married seven years and had no children, I could not imagine life without my husband, brother, and father. If Michael died, I really didn't think I could go on. As tragic as Josiah's death was, I knew I couldn't lose two men dear to me. Losing Michael too would have put me in my grave."

Julia wiped at her own tears. "How awful that must have been."

Anna appreciated the commiseration. "I turned everything over to the Lord. I told Him I would do whatever He asked if He'd only spare my brother. I told the Lord I would serve Him the remainder of my days in exchange for my brother's life." Even now, so many years later, she remembered the utter desperation she'd felt, later followed by the sweet and miraculous blessing of her brother making a full recovery.

"With every day that Michael lived," she continued, "it was a blessing and a triumph. He went on to live a full life, as you know. His death a few years ago was something I both grieved and rejoiced over. Grief that he was gone, but joy that he'd been spared at a young age. And you are a result of his posterity. I couldn't be more grateful to have you in my home now." She smiled at her great-niece.

Julia sniffled and tried to smile back. "I didn't realize all that you promised the Lord on my grandfather's behalf, and I didn't know the impact you had on his life."

"How could you, my dear?" Anna asked. "The only person I told about it was my own father. He's been gone these many years."

"My grandfather talked often about his own father," Julia mused. "I wish I could have met him."

Anna was touched by the young woman's sincerity. "My father, Phanuel, would have been proud of you."

At this comment, Julia's expression fell. "I don't know about that. I can't even please my parents."

Anna's heart tugged at her great-niece's plight. Yet, years of working and serving in the temple and edging her way through the many trials of life had taught her that God was the supreme ruler and He could work miracles.

"Be patient, and wait for the answers from God," Anna said. "I know it's difficult, yet I am living proof of patience."

"Thank you," Julia said softly. "Having you share your story has helped me more than you know."

"I'm so glad," Anna said. "Come now, we must get rest. Tomorrow will be a busy day at the temple, and I want you to accompany me. I hope to introduce you to Simeon. His story will also strengthen your faith."

Julia rose to her feet, and Anna followed. The two women embraced, and Anna felt as if she had had a piece of her past restored to her. Michael's blood ran through Julia's veins, and it was good to have family with her once again.

The following morning, Anna rose with the sun. Despite the lateness of the hour when she'd gone to bed after talking well into the night with Julia, Anna wasn't about to break her habits. Dawn had always urged her to begin her day.

Today, the aches throughout her body seemed more pronounced. It was probably due to the trip to the market, followed by the meal at Cyria's, and then having a shorter rest. Regardless, Anna prepared the morning meal on her own, giving Julia the extra sleep she surely needed and deserved. Anna hoped that she'd be able to help Julia understand the great importance of her family and, in turn, praying for the Lord's guidance in all things.

"Let me help you, Aunt," Julia's voice came from the other side of the room as she entered.

Anna looked up from setting bowls on the table. "Thank you. Did you sleep well?"

Julia fought back a yawn. "I slept well enough, but it appears as if you were up early again. I feel lazy compared to you."

"You are far from lazy," Anna said. "I have a hard time breaking my routine. But last night's conversation was worth a little missed sleep. Thank you for listening."

Julia nodded and smiled. "I am amazed by your story, and I'm looking forward to visiting the temple today."

"Wonderful," Anna said. "The meal is ready, and then we'll begin our journey."

The two women ate boiled grain in relative silence, and then they set off. The day was overcast but balmy, and Julia doubted it would rain. Regardless, they were prepared with their mantles.

As they walked, Anna saw that the early risers were already moving about the sprawl of the city. Vendors were setting up their carts of wares along the edges of the market square, and Anna noticed that Julia kept her eyes peeled for Philip. However, neither Philip nor his brother were to be seen. Only a couple of merchants were actively selling bread to other merchants setting up to begin a day of selling at the market.

When they reached the holy mount, the eastern gate loomed before them, and Anna led Julia through the gate into the Court of the Gentiles. She'd been here several days a week for years, but walking with Julia gave Anna a new outlook. The court was paved with stones of different colors, which were quite beautiful in the morning light. A couple of money-changers had already set up for the day, and a cattle-dealer was hustling men coming to the temple.

Anna continued past the pillars inscribed with Latin, Greek, and Hebrew that warned the Gentiles to walk no farther, to stay out of the Court of Women. The east side was comprised of a wide wall etched with a beautiful sculpture of the city of Susa and the Gate Beautiful. Anna led Julia toward the Court of Women, where they'd spend most of their time. Columns and the thirteen treasure chests outlined the small area. Beyond the Court of Women was the semicircular staircase leading to the Nicanor Gate. And then finally, the Court of the Priests, where women weren't allowed. It was possible, though, to look over the balcony to see the ceremonies in the inner court.

Julia was wide-eyed as she looked about the huge place.

"Take this shawl and cover your head," Anna said, handing her a prayer shawl reserved for the women who came to worship and pray. Anna had made the shawls herself over the years and took home any that needed to be cleaned or repaired.

People had already formed a line, coming through the Gate Beautiful, bringing their sin or peace offerings. One couple, carrying an infant, had brought a lamb for a purification sacrifice.

After their prayers were finished, Anna looked about for Simeon. He came to the temple every few days, and Anna hoped that today would be one of those days. She didn't see him inside the temple complex though, so she looked outside of it from her position. When she spotted him, her heart soared. He was resting in the shade of some palm trees. She didn't know whether he was leaving the temple or arriving, but she wanted to take the opportunity to speak to him where it was quieter.

"I've located Simeon," she told Julia. "Let's go speak with him. I think you'll find his story remarkable."

Julia replaced her prayer shawl in the basket at the entrance to the Court of Women. The two women walked out of the court and across the temple grounds, where more and more people had arrived, bustling with activity. They passed through the gate, pleased to see that Simeon hadn't left his spot in the shade.

"Simeon," Anna called out, and he turned his head. His shoulders sloped forward with age, his skin was deeply wrinkled, but his brown eyes were bright and intelligent. "I've brought someone to meet you."

After Anna made introductions, Simeon gave a regal nod to Julia.

"Welcome to Jerusalem," he said. "You are in good hands with Anna." He turned his eager gaze back to Anna. "Did you see the new star?"

Anna smiled. "We did see it. Julia came with me, and we watched it burn brightly."

"What do you think it means?" Simeon asked. "Do we dare hope the new star is a sign of the Messiah's birth?"

His words echoed Anna's hopes, and she felt a warmth spread through her. "I believe it is." For how much longer could Simeon live? She guessed him to be nearly a century in age. She was grateful to be able to speak of the star with someone who had such great faith.

Julia was watching and listening closely, another thing Anna was grateful for.

"Come and stand in the shade," Simeon said, gesturing to a space beside him. "The day grows hotter by the moment."

Anna and Julia joined the man, and Simeon wasted no more time before speaking to Julia. "Did Anna tell you about the promise revealed to me by the Holy Spirit?" he asked in a hushed voice.

Julia's smile was sweet and genuine, and this further warmed Anna's heart. The young woman was proving to be an eager student.

Although there were people passing by them on the way to the temple gate, standing beneath the shade of the palm afforded them a measure of privacy.

"The Holy Spirit promised that I would not see death until I have seen the Messiah," Simeon said in a hushed voice. "And look at me. I am an old man. This means that the Messiah will be coming soon."

Every time Anna heard Simeon talk about his experience, she felt a rush of warmth across her skin. Their gazes connected, and Simeon moved a step closer. "Perhaps it has already happened."

Julia looked at Anna as if to find out what she thought about Simeon's pronouncement.

Anna gave a nod, and this seemed to encourage Simeon to speak more. "Have you heard of the miraculous birth of Zacharias's son?" Simeon asked, looking at Julia.

"Who is Zacharias?"

"Come," Simeon answered, motioning toward a grouping of rocks. "We will sit, out of the way of other listeners, and I will tell you about a miraculous birth."

Anna and Julia followed, and Anna was grateful that Julia would hear the story. Simeon was at the temple the day Zacharias had been struck dumb after having a vision in the Inner Court. The story would be better coming straight from Simeon.

Anna didn't know Zacharias or his wife, but when she heard what had happened, she believed it completely.

After they'd settled on the rocks, Simeon clasped his hands together. The breeze stirred about Anna's feet, bringing relief of cooler air, but it also made her sense that even the elements were listening and affirming Simeon's account as he began his story.

"Over a year ago—perhaps nearly fifteen moons now—the priest Zacharias was at the temple, burning the incense, as was his duty that day," Simeon said in a soft tone, as if he were reliving the scene at that exact moment. "Zacharias was in the Inner Court when an angel appeared before him. I was outside the Inner Court when Zacharias came out. I have never seen a man look such as he did that day."

CHAPTER
TWENTY

"How did Zacharias look that day?" Julia asked when Simeon said that Zacharias was a changed man. Simeon's story was mesmerizing, and Julia marveled at all he said.

Simeon didn't seem to mind the interruption. "The priest's eyes had a new depth, and his skin was so pale that it was almost white. Most importantly, he could not speak a word. We all knew something remarkable had happened to him. Although we wouldn't find out the whole story until many months later, after the birth of his son, John."

Julia shifted her position to better face Simeon. "Did his son's birth have something to do with the visit from the angel?"

"Oh yes," Simeon said with a smile. "For you see, his wife, Elisabeth, was barren and well past her childbearing years. The angel told Zacharias that his wife would conceive and bring forth a son."

Julia glanced at Anna, and her aunt nodded. "It would be like me conceiving at my age—if Josiah had lived this long."

That would be a true miracle, indeed, Julia decided.

Simeon continued, a smile on his face. "As you can imagine, Zacharias was more than surprised by the angel's pronouncement. In fact, he argued with the angel."

"How do you argue with an angel?" Julia asked.

"That's what I wondered as well," Anna said, laughter in her voice.

"Zacharias did," Simeon said. "And the Lord made him mute until his son was born. At that time, his speech was restored, and he was able to testify of all he'd seen and heard."

Julia tried to imagine Elisabeth's reaction to her husband's affliction and then the subsequent birth of a child in her old age. "How old is the child now?"

Simeon glanced at Anna, and she answered, "I would say John is in his fifth month. I saw Elisabeth at the temple with her purification sacrifice when the babe was forty days old. Since then, I've seen her a time or two at the market. She doesn't venture far on account of her age."

"I saw Zacharias at the temple today," Simeon announced.

Both Julia and Anna looked at him in surprise.

"He's not working this month," Simeon clarified. "I saw him bring in a sin offering early this morning."

"Do you think he's still here?" Julia asked, marveling that she might get a chance to see a man who'd experienced such a miracle and conversed with an angel.

"Most likely," Simeon said, smiling at her. It was as if he guessed her next question. "I would be happy to point him out to you if I see him again."

"Was his wife with him?" Julia asked.

"No," Simeon said. "You might visit her at her home."

"I couldn't do that," Julia began, but Anna interrupted.

"Perhaps we shall." She linked her arm through Julia's and told Simeon, "We best be on our way. Thank you for sharing your story, Simeon. We have been well fed this day."

Simeon nodded and bade them farewell.

As Anna led Julia away from the man and away from the temple complex, Julia asked, "Where are we going? And why did we leave so abruptly?"

Anna was silent for a moment as they passed by several travelers heading toward the temple. "I have had an idea, and I want to see it through before I lose the courage."

"What is it?" Julia pressed. They were nearing the market, and she kept her eyes open for Philip.

"I think we shall visit Elisabeth, if she is home," Anna said.

"Really?" Julia asked. "Do you know her?"

"I don't know her personally, but she might know of me," Anna said. "I hope she will welcome us into her home. I'd love to hear her story firsthand."

"I would too," Julia said, her interest piqued at the thought of talking to the older woman who had once been barren until a miracle occurred. "Do you think she will talk to us?" Julia asked.

"Her husband has made no secret of his experience," Anna said. "So I don't see why his wife wouldn't be welcoming and forthcoming as well."

Julia smiled to herself. Just then, she spotted Philip and Seth speaking to a man who looked a lot like Bartholomew. Upon closer inspection, she realized it was Bartholomew. She tightened her hold on Anna's arm. "Is there another way we can go and not bypass the blacksmiths' stand?"

"What is wrong?" Anna asked immediately.

"The man who Philip is speaking with . . . that's Bartholomew."

Anna didn't need any more explanation, and she steered Julia to the right. They walked along an open alley between a group of one-story buildings until they reached another road.

"Is it far?" Julia asked, wondering if the walk was going to tire Anna.

"It's a little way," Anna said. "But if we aren't received by Elisabeth, we'll wait awhile so we won't have to walk back in the heat of the day."

Nearly an hour later, they entered a neighborhood with small homes and square courtyards. Each courtyard was well-tended, and Julia sensed that a lot of pride went into these modest homes.

A young girl came out of one of the courtyards, shooing two goats in front of her. They started to run at an awkward pace, and she followed, laughing. When she drew near, her curious gaze locked on Julia.

"Can you tell us where Elisabeth, Zachariah's wife, lives?" Anna asked the girl.

She nodded and pointed down the road. "The house with the two fountains."

"Thank you," Anna said.

The girl chased after her goats again, her bare feet tripping on the dirt road as she ran. The day had grown quite warm, and Julia hoped Elisabeth would offer them some water as well.

They approached a home that did, indeed, have two fountains in the front courtyard. Several stately palms provided cooling shade, and Anna seemed to appreciate the break from the heat as well. Julia and Anna stood outside the gate, and Anna invited Julia to call out for Elisabeth. They didn't dare enter the gate and cross the courtyard since they hadn't been introduced.

"Hello? Elisabeth?" Julia said in a raised voice.

Moments later, a woman who looked to be a servant scurried out of the house. She was perhaps Julia's age.

"Elisabeth asks who her visitors are," the woman said.

"You may tell her it's Anna from the temple and her great-niece. We are friends of Simeon."

The servant nodded, then crossed the courtyard and disappeared into the house.

Julia glanced at Anna when the servant was gone. "At least she's home."

"Yes," Anna said. "All we can do now is hope she'll receive us."

When the servant returned, she opened the gate. "Follow me," she said, leading them across the courtyard and then around the house.

Julia didn't know what it meant when they weren't invited inside the house. But when they reached the back courtyard, she saw that staying outside would be a much better option than a stuffy house.

The back courtyard had nearly a dozen palms surrounding a pool of water. Flowers and grass grew along the narrow banks, and not only did the water and shade create a cool setting, but the flowers were sweetly fragrant too. Beyond the pool, a garden stretched out, the plants young and green. On the other side of the garden plot, a tangle of vines and bushes grew like a protective barrier between the courtyard and the next house behind.

The servant led them to a long bench and asked them to sit.

"I will bring you refreshment, and my mistress will join you soon," the servant said.

"Well," Anna said after the servant disappeared again. "This is unexpected, but very, very welcome."

Julia smiled her agreement.

In the next moment, another woman came out of the house. She had a babe bundled to her chest, and her hair was streaked with silver.

Julia felt compelled to stand as the woman approached.

Her gaze was sharp as she looked from Julia to Anna, then her eyes softened in recognition. "I have seen you at the temple," the woman said in a voice raspy with age.

Anna rose next to Julia and held out her hand. "We are sorry for the intrusion. This is my great-niece Julia. She is descended from my brother."

"I am Elisabeth," the woman said, grasping Anna's hand. Their touch was brief, then Elisabeth let go. "My babe is called John." Her gaze shifted to Julia. "I am sure my husband knows your family. He remembers everyone's name. Me, not as much. You must sit and have refreshment. It is a warm day."

"Thank you," Anna said, reiterated by Julia.

They retook their seats on the bench, and Elisabeth sat near them. "John has been fussy this week," she said. "I have taken to binding him against me, and he seems much calmer when I do."

"Perhaps he is growing a tooth?" Anna said.

Elisabeth smiled, and Julia could see how she must have been a beautiful woman in her youth. She was still beautiful. Age had been kind, adding wrinkles, but otherwise, she was striking even with her faded hair color. Yet Julia well knew that beauty would never outrank the ability to have children. Barrenness was considered a curse from God and a reason for some men to put away their wives.

"I do think John is growing a tooth." Elisabeth stroked her sleeping son's head. His dark curls were abundant, even at such a young age.

The servant came out of the house, bearing a tray of cups and a platter of fresh fruit. Julia's mouth watered at the sight.

Elisabeth graciously thanked the servant, then handed a cup each to Anna and Julia.

Julia sipped at the liquid, surprised to taste a fruit juice. It was sweet and delicious, and she had to force herself not to drink it all down in a few swallows.

"What has brought you to my home?" Elisabeth asked after she'd inquired about Julia's family and Anna's health.

Anna cleared her throat. "Earlier today, I introduced Julia to the old man Simeon, who shared his tale with her."

"Ah, do you mean the story of how he will live to see the Messiah?" Elisabeth asked.

Julia couldn't decipher her tone—she spoke lightly, yet there was no mocking in her voice.

"Yes," Anna said carefully. "I have heard his story many times, and I wanted Julia to hear it for herself," Anna continued. "After sharing his own experiences, Simeon then told Julia of Zacharias's experience in the Inner Court when he saw an angel." She took a deep breath, as if she'd had to force out the words all at once.

Elisabeth picked up her cup and took a sip of her juice. Then she set it down in a deliberate manner. "I am sure there are many variations of Zacharias's story spread about. It was many months, more than nine months, before he could tell the story himself. So as you can imagine, there was much speculation created."

Anna folded her hands in her lap and nodded. Julia watched Elisabeth closely and determined that the woman seemed a bit reluctant to explain. Julia hoped Elisabeth would feel safe to share more.

"We are not here to question or censure," Anna said, reaching out and patting Elisabeth on the arm. "I, too, have witnessed miracles in my lifetime. There is a reason I have remained a widow seven years from my virginity and have served in the temple these past decades."

Elisabeth seemed to consider that for a few moments. She picked up a piece of melon and took a bite. Then she swallowed, and said, "I know of your faith and devotion, Anna. I have thought you someone who might have had no other choice in life. I don't mean to offend; this is merely idle gossip. But meeting you, I sense you are a woman who lives by the light from heaven in all things."

Anna brushed away tears, and Julia realized tears had formed in her own eyes.

"Thank you," Anna said quietly.

"If there's one thing my husband's experience and the birth of our son so late in life has taught me, it's to never assume you know anything about another person's life." Elisabeth placed a hand on her babe's back as if she were protecting him from something. "When my husband came home from the temple that day, I could not understand what had happened."

Julia tried to imagine such a scenario herself.

"I wanted to call the healer, but he kept shaking his head no and putting his hands together as if in prayer," Elisabeth said, her eyes bright with memory. "It took some adjustment to live in a house with a mute and deaf husband. When I mimed to him later that I was with child, he wept. I thought, of course, that he was pleased. It wasn't until he wrote down what had happened with the angel's pronouncement that I understood everything."

"John looks to be a healthy boy," Anna said.

As if John had heard Anna speak his name, he stirred in his wrapped cocoon.

"He's been a dear child," Elisabeth said. "Not that I've had experience with another, but I have enjoyed every minute with him.

I was so surprised and so afraid when I found out I was with child. My advanced age is no small factor."

"You have come through it well," Anna said in a soothing voice. "How is your health?"

"I am healthy enough," Elisabeth said. "I have hired a servant to help with some of the cleaning and cooking since little John takes much of my energy throughout the day and night." She smiled down at the sleeping child. "I wouldn't trade him for anything though. If I had to make do without a servant, I'd find a way."

"He's a beautiful child," Anna continued. "We are blessed to see him."

Elisabeth's attention went to Anna. "Have you heard the rest of the story, then?"

Julia looked between the women, unsure of what they were speaking about.

"I have heard some of it but not in its entirety," Anna said in a soft voice.

Elisabeth rubbed a hand over her son's head, then released a sigh. "I have told few people because the first friend I told ended up turning against me. I guess I was hesitant after that. I told my cousin Mary . . . who visited me when I was in my fifth month."

Anna reached out a hand. "We are not asking you to confide. I brought my niece Julia so that she might learn of John's miraculous birth firsthand, but she already understands the first miracle of it."

Elisabeth smiled at Anna, then looked at Julia.

Julia swallowed, not sure if she should say anything since she wasn't exactly sure what the women were speaking about in the first place.

"John is a special child," Elisabeth said in a quiet voice, keeping her gaze on Julia. "He's a chosen child."

CHAPTER TWENTY-ONE

HE'S A CHOSEN CHILD, ELISABETH had said about John. And Julia knew the woman wasn't speaking the words lightly. Julia felt goose flesh rise on the back of her neck. Was Elisabeth about to claim that the infant in her arms was the Messiah? She sent a panicked look at Anna, but her aunt's face was serene, as if she accepted every word Elisabeth spoke.

"When the angel spoke to Zacharias in the temple," Elisabeth continued, recapturing Julia's attention, "he told Zacharias that his son would be great in the sight of the Lord."

Julia nodded. This was a blessing pronounced upon infants by rabbis frequently. Every child had the potential to be great in the eyes of the Lord.

"The angel told my husband that our son would be born before the Messiah and would prepare the people for His arrival," Elisabeth said in a low voice. "The angel said that our son will have the spirit and power of Elias to turn the hearts of the fathers to their children. Our son will become an instrument to convince the disobedient to become righteous and just."

Something in Julia's heart fluttered, and for some reason, her eyes burned with tears. Could this be true? Could the child in Elisabeth's arms be a prophet?

Anna spoke next. "I have heard some of these things, and it's a beautiful promise and blessing."

Sitting out here in this peaceful garden, Julia felt Elisabeth's words burrow their way into her heart. Julia couldn't quite explain how she felt, just that she felt somehow content, as if her worries over mundane things and even important things were not such great worries after all. If John was a prophet to prepare the way for God's Messiah, that meant the Messiah would be born in the child's lifetime. Perhaps as soon as a few years or even a couple of decades. Which meant that the Messiah could very well be born in Julia's lifetime. The thought was staggering to consider.

"Have you seen the new star?" Elisabeth asked.

"Yes," Anna said. "Julia and I watched it the other night. What do you think about it?"

Elisabeth focused on her sleeping babe for a moment, then lifted her gaze. "There are other things that have happened that I have kept close to my heart. Only Zacharias knows of them."

Julia leaned closer, not wanting to miss a word Elisabeth spoke.

"When I was in my fifth month of being with child, my young cousin Mary came to visit me." Elisabeth blew out a slow breath, her eyes watering.

Julia wondered if something was wrong, if something terrible had happened to the woman named Mary.

"Mary traveled from her home in Nazareth to come visit me," Elisabeth continued. "She was young, unmarried, and with child."

Julia hid her gasp. Was Elisabeth about to tell them her cousin had become an outcast or been stoned? Julia had heard of such awful stories.

"When Mary came to my doorstep, I was surprised to see her since there had been no word of her traveling to see me. I did not know of her condition when I first greeted her, but I still wouldn't have turned her away if I had." Elisabeth's voice grew even more quiet. "The babe in my womb leapt with joy, and I was flooded with the Spirit of the Lord and with a knowledge of—" Her voice broke, and she closed her eyes for a moment.

When Elisabeth opened her eyes again, tears spilled onto her cheeks. "My own babe, my son, knew about the child Mary was carrying. *My babe leapt in my womb.* Without a word from Mary, the Holy Spirit testified to me that she was carrying the Messiah and that she is the mother of our Lord."

Julia stared at Elisabeth. It seemed all the sounds of the garden had faded into silence, and Julia couldn't speak, couldn't even form a question to ask.

Anna grasped Elisabeth's hand. "Even before his birth, John was a witness of the Messiah."

Elisabeth wiped at her tears with her other hand. "This is a sacred experience to me, and I hope you will understand."

Julia's own eyes were burning with tears again. She didn't exactly understand all that was being said, but if Mary was newly with child when she visited Elisabeth, that meant the babes were about six months apart. Julia looked at the sleeping child strapped to Elisabeth's torso. Was his cousin born already?

When Julia met Elisabeth's gaze, it was as if the woman knew what she was thinking.

"Mary should be delivered very soon, if she hasn't already," Elisabeth said.

The first thought that went through Julia's mind was: *the new star.* Was it possible? Had the Messiah been born? It seemed that Anna was thinking the same thing.

"Surely the new star is a sign of Mary's delivery of the Messiah?" Anna said quietly. "How soon will you hear news from Nazareth?"

Elisabeth wiped at a fresh round of tears. "Mary sent word that she was going to Bethlehem with Joseph, her husband."

Julia blinked back her surprise.

Elisabeth explained. "Joseph was Mary's betrothed. She spent three months with me, then had to return to her family to explain what had happened. It seems that Joseph did not put her away."

"What a blessing," Anna murmured.

For a man to discover his betrothed was with child and not put her away was astounding indeed, Julia thought.

Elisabeth nodded. "Mary told me she'd been visited by an angel." Her smile was tremulous. "Much like my Zacharias. The angel appeared to Mary and told her she was highly favored, and she was blessed among women."

Julia tried to imagine such an event. How would she react to the sight of an angel?

"The angel told Mary she would conceive in her womb and bring forth a son and call him Jesus," Elisabeth said.

"Jesus," Julia whispered to herself.

Anna wiped tears from her face. "Your cousin Mary is a virgin?"

"Yes," Elisabeth whispered.

Anna shook her head in wonder. "Then it is like the prophet Isaiah said: 'Therefore the Lord himself shall give you a sign; Behold, a virgin shall conceive, and bear a son, and shall call his name Immanuel.'"

Julia was well familiar with Isaiah's prophecies about a special person favored of the Lord. She'd heard about them many times.

Elisabeth nodded and wiped at her own tears. "The angel told Mary that her son would be great and called the Son of the Highest. Her son would reign over the house of Jacob forever, and his kingdom would have no end."

Both Anna and Julia remained silent as Elisabeth said, "Mary asked how she might conceive since she was a virgin. The angel told her that the power of the Holy Spirit would come upon her and the power of the Highest would overshadow her. The angel also told Mary that I was with child and in my fifth month."

"So Mary came to visit you, knowing that you would understand," Anna said.

"Yes." Elisabeth turned her watery eyes upon Anna. "I have been praying for her every day since she left. Joseph had to go to Bethlehem to pay taxes, and Mary said she was going with him. I don't know the outcome of the journey or if they are back in Nazareth now."

"Bethlehem?" Anna said, her voice sounding incredulous.

Elisabeth furrowed her brow. "Is something wrong?"

"The prophet Micah has said that the Messiah will be born in Bethlehem."

Julia stared at her aunt as goose flesh rose upon her arms.

Elisabeth smiled. "I must tell my husband when he returns home from the temple."

"Surely he knows of the prophecy," Anna said.

"He must know. And he will be pleased to know that there is a chance Mary and Joseph are still in Bethlehem," Elisabeth said, grasping Anna's hand. "Thank you, my dear friend."

It took Julia awhile to sort through what Elisabeth and Anna had said. There were so many miracles and amazing occurrences. Had the Messiah been born in Bethlehem as the prophets had foretold? And had the new star been a sign of the day of his birth?

With all these wonders competing for comprehension in her mind, her problems with her parents and Bartholomew seemed but trivial and earthly concerns.

She and Anna spent another couple of hours with Elisabeth. When little John awakened, Julia took a turn in holding the bright-eyed infant. If there was anything she could say about the child, it was that he seemed intelligent beyond his age. Just looking into his eyes made Julia feel like this child was truly a chosen being. She marveled that an angel had foretold his birth and that his arrival was such a miracle in and of itself.

Elisabeth invited them to stay for a meal. Zacharias would not be home for a few days, and the women ate together. The more Julia learned about Elisabeth, and the more she heard about Mary, the more convinced she was that they were deeply spiritual women thriving on a wealth of faith.

When the afternoon began to fade into evening, Anna declared that they would need to start back home. So it was amid kisses and embraces that Julia and Anna bade farewell to Elisabeth. She made both of them promise to visit again.

"If Mary's child has been born, she will be attending the temple for purification within forty days," Elisabeth said. "She may be staying at my home for the event. I can only hope."

Julia didn't know if she would still be living with Anna in forty days, but suddenly, she wanted to make sure she was.

As Julia walked down the road with Anna on the way back to her neighborhood, she marveled at all that had taken place. The sun had settled against the western horizon, bringing relief from the heat, and the journey went much quicker than before. Julia was so wrapped up in her thoughts, she didn't even think to look about the market square to see if Philip and his brother were closing up for the day.

It was nearly dark by the time they reached Anna's home, and Julia did some chores about the house by the light of a couple of oil lamps while Anna rested. When Julia was finished, she found Anna sitting on the cushions in the gathering room.

"Come and sit awhile," Anna said, extending her hand.

Julia joined her great-aunt and pulled a small rug over both of them.

"What did you think about Elisabeth's story?" Anna asked.

Julia exhaled. "It made me feel like a selfish woman."

Anna gave a small chuckle. "Why do you say that?"

"Hearing about Elisabeth's life and about her cousin Mary and all they have been dealing with has shown me that I have kept my eyes on earthly concerns," Julia said in a quiet voice. "I have put my own wants before everyone else in my family, and I have forgotten the meaning of my life."

Anna patted her hand. "It's not as dire as all that, is it?"

"Just as you told me earlier, I need to live by more faith," Julia said. "I have tried to change minds and show defiance in order to get my way, when in fact, if I were a humble and prayerful woman, such as Elisabeth, I would enjoy more peace."

"I can agree with that," Anna said.

Julia leaned her head back against the cool wall. "I can't force my parents to accept my decision. They have their own right to make their decision, and I know they want what's best for me. They are protecting me by telling me to not marry someone like Philip. They don't want their own daughter ostracized, even though that shouldn't happen in the first place. I can accept that is the way of life in our village."

"It's unfortunate," Anna said. "But with the birth of the Messiah, He will teach us how to live in peace."

Julia was silent for a moment. "I cannot believe these events have been foretold for centuries, and they are happening now. It seems that Simeon was right."

"Simeon *was* right." Anna agreed. "He will live to see the Messiah. And it's a marvel to realize the Messiah has been born at last."

These words sent a shiver of warmth through Julia. Could it be true that the Son of the Almighty was a small infant only a short distance from Jerusalem? That He'd been born to His mother, Mary, and even now, was living, breathing, and would someday redeem the world? "Will we see Him, do you think?" Julia asked reverently.

"If the Lord allows me to live until the days of Mary's purification, then we will see him." Anna looked over at Julia. "We need to make sure you are still here as well."

"If my father comes to collect me, what will we tell him?" Julia asked. "Do we share what Elisabeth has told us?"

"We will decide when that moment comes," Anna said, lowering her voice. "Elisabeth's story isn't for everyone. There will be some who will not believe it and who will taunt her for it. But you have seen the miracle of John's life for yourself."

Julia blinked back the tears forming in her eyes. "I cannot deny what I have seen. I also cannot deny what I have heard and felt. I have never felt so much peace and assurance before that there is a God in heaven looking over all of us. Sending the Messiah to earth only shows how much He cares for us."

"It has been a remarkable day," Anna said, giving a tremulous smile. "I have lived many, many years, and I have never experienced such wonder as I have today. We are blessed to be witnesses."

CHAPTER TWENTY-TWO

JULIA SPENT THE NEXT THIRTY days with Anna, helping her clean, cook, care for her garden, and visit the temple. She and Anna listened for any word of a birth in Bethlehem by a woman named Mary. They spoke to Simeon. Anna even pointed out Zacharias one time from afar.

All this, while Julia waited and wondered. When would the days of purification be completed for Mary, and would Julia be able to see the Messiah herself?

One day, she was finally able to speak with Philip alone. She'd taken Anna to the market and had spotted Philip and his brother right away. When Julia was looking at a cart of jars of honey and bunches of dried spices, Philip came up next to her.

"You have been busy," he said in a low voice, a voice that Julia knew so well.

She could picture his brown eyes before she turned and looked at him. "I have been helping Anna more and more."

Philip nodded, a slight smile on his face as he studied her. "You are well?"

"I am." Her breath felt light as it always did around him. Today, he wore a pale-brown tunic that contrasted with his dark hair and dark eyes. She also noticed his scent of spice, along with the musk that a working man exuded. "How is business for you and your brother?"

"We could work day and night and still have work," Philip said.

Julia didn't doubt it. Their booth was always surrounded by customers, and every time she spotted Philip, he was either working or speaking with a customer. "This has been a successful season, then," she said.

Philip's smile grew wider. "Yes. I have been saving almost everything I've earned. We are even sleeping on the ground to save on lodging."

Her heart thumped because she sensed what he was going to say next.

"Can we talk by the well?"

Julia knew the location. It was where the merchants filled their goatskins with water in order to continue working through the heat of the day. Right now, the cloud cover had given reprieve from the heat, and only two people seemed to be near the well.

"All right." Julia set down the jar of honey that she'd been holding and made her way through the crowd toward the well. Philip followed, although he didn't walk as if they were traveling together. That was probably wise, Julia decided.

When she reached the well, the people who had been there had already left, so Julia busied herself by lowering the goatskin bucket into the well.

Philip joined her as she was pulling up the bucket. His arm brushed hers as he reached for the bucket and drew it the rest of the way out.

"Are you thirsty?" he asked.

If she hadn't been before, she was now. Being around Philip always made her warm. He produced a cup from his satchel and poured water into it, then handed it over to her. She took a sip of the cool liquid, then handed it back. He took his own sip of the water.

"We return to the village next week," Philip said, setting the cup on the edge of the well.

"So soon?" Julia said before she could think about it. She'd been here several weeks, and so had Philip. In truth, she hadn't expected the opportunity to see him as much as she had, although they'd talked only on the day they'd had a meal at Cyria's.

"Seth needs to return to his family, and business will slow down over the next few days," Philip said.

His eyes were intent on hers, and she felt her face heat up at the attention. She leaned against the edge of the well and looked down at her hands.

"Have you thought more about what we spoke about earlier?" he asked in a low voice.

"I have." She'd thought about it every day. She'd thought about *him* every day. "I have been learning a lot living with Anna." She hesitated, wondering how much she should, or could, share with Philip. When she looked up, though, she saw nothing but interest in his eyes . . . and hope.

"What is it?" Philip asked. "If you are to turn me down, I would never hold it against you. I would understand."

He stepped closer, then leaned against the well wall next to her. If she moved just a little, their arms would brush.

"Like you said, it's not a simple matter," Julia said. "There's no doubt in my heart that I want to be your wife. And there's no doubt I would be happy with you."

One side of his mouth lifted into a smile, but she could see the wariness in his gaze.

"I've made a decision, Philip." Her pulse pounded, and she hoped she'd have the courage to follow through with what she wanted to say. "I want to make peace with my parents, and I want to tell them the desires of my heart—all my desires—so that they understand what I feel for you. I want to explain to them that I want to change the hearts of the villagers about your family. I believe if my family embraces your family, we can change those hearts."

Philip opened his mouth as if to speak, then he looked as if he couldn't find the words. After a few moments, he said, "You would do that for me?"

"Yes," she whispered. She wanted to take his hand and reassure him, but they were in a public place.

"What if your parents don't agree to help you change the villagers' hearts?" he finally asked, as she knew he would. "What if they are too afraid to be different?"

Julia exhaled. "I have thought of this too. I will be sharing all that I've learned about the temple and about God. I believe God would want His children to treat each other with kindness. To learn to get along better." She felt her eyes well up with tears. Philip and his siblings had no part in their mother's desertion. "If my parents are absolutely against us, then I will abide by their decision. Although I will not marry another. How can I when my heart is yours?"

Philip rubbed at his face, and Julia saw that there were tears in his eyes as well. "You can't promise not to marry, Julia. I understand if you want to remain in your parents' good graces. But you don't want to give up the chance to have your own family."

"There is much to be done in life that doesn't include bearing children," Julia said. "I'm sure my parents didn't think my mind would lead me to that conclusion when they sent me to live with Anna. Spending time with her, I've found the true meaning of love and peace. It's not through disassociating yourself with people in your life. It's through forgiveness and love."

"You're wise beyond your years," Philip said, his hand brushing hers. "If only the rest of us could be so compassionate."

"I believe a great change is coming," Julia said, her heart expanding. "I can't explain everything now, but Anna and I have been witnesses to signs of the Messiah."

Philip's brows shot up. "What signs?"

Because he sounded interested and not disbelieving, and because Julia hoped one day to marry this man, she told him about the new star Anna had pointed out. She told him about Simeon, and she told him about Zacharias and Elisabeth and John. As she spoke, she realized all the people she was speaking about were ones she admired greatly, and they all had one thing in common—their love and devotion to God. Julia wanted to be like that—like them. She wanted to put God first, to put others first, and to not dwell on her own trials. When she finished telling her stories to Philip, he looked deep in thought.

When he did meet her gaze, Julia saw determination there. "I would like to meet Simeon. I will speak to my brother, and perhaps I can take a half day to go to the temple."

A thrill ran through Julia at his pronouncement. "We can speak to Anna about when the best time is."

He nodded. "How many days did you say it has been since the new star appeared?"

"Thirty-two days." She could almost imagine what he was thinking.

His gaze connected with hers. "The purification sacrifice could be in a week." He straightened from his position and looked down at Julia. "What do you think about me speaking to your father when I return to the village?"

Julia hesitated at this. She appreciated Philip's willingness, but she also didn't want him to be mistreated. She just didn't know what her father's reaction would be. "I think I'd like to speak to my parents first. I don't know what their response will be."

Although Philip looked like he might argue, he said, "All right. I will wait until you feel the time is right."

A woman approached the well, with a couple of children trailing after her. Julia and Philip's private conversation was about to be interrupted.

Philip stepped away from Julia, a look of regret in his eyes, as if he'd wanted to say more to her. Julia smiled at him to assure him that she would do her best with her parents. She was at peace, knowing that she was taking the right course. Her experiences with Anna were teaching Julia that she needed to trust more in the Lord. He knew her burdens, and He would help her. She had to believe that.

Julia watched Philip walk away and rejoin his brother, then she made her way to Anna, who was speaking with another woman.

"Are you ready to return home?" Anna asked when she saw Julia.

"Yes," Julia said, and after Anna bade farewell to her friend, they left the market.

As they neared Anna's home, Julia immediately knew something was different. A cart sat in front of the courtyard, and a man was unloading some things from it. *Father*.

"Good heavens," Anna murmured, echoing Julia's thoughts exactly. "Silas is here."

It was as if her father had heard Anna, and he turned to see the women approach.

Julia's heart thumped with worry. Her father wasn't exactly smiling, nor did he look pleased to see her.

Anna squeezed Julia's hand, then let go. "Hello, Silas," she greeted her nephew. "Welcome back to Jerusalem. Would you like some refreshment?"

"That would be welcome." He glanced at Julia.

She couldn't read his expression. Why was he here? Had he finally decided to force his decision on her, or was he in Jerusalem for some other reason?

She stepped forward to kiss him on the cheek.

When she drew away, he said, "I have news. Let's go inside." He hauled out a basket of olives from the cart. "I've brought these from my grove."

Anna thanked him for the olives, and the three of them entered her home. Julia helped Anna store the olives, then prepared drink and refreshment, though, really, they should have prepared a meal. All the while, Julia's impatience and dread made her feel like she'd swallowed a rock.

When they were settled in the gathering room, Julia's father began. "Our neighbor reported that Philip and Seth have been in

Jerusalem working at the market this past month. I did not think much about it until your mother said that you had asked after him a few months ago."

Julia's face heated, and she could only nod. Her father didn't seem as angry as she thought he might at this news. He was also waiting for a reply. She glanced at her aunt, then said to her father, "I have feelings for Philip, and I brought his name up to Mother because I knew that many in the village have distanced themselves from Philip's family on account of his mother's actions."

Her father didn't reply, so Julia continued, taking some comfort that Anna was in the room. "If the actions of Philip's mother are the only objection you and Mother have against Philip, I would like to see if that concern can be allayed," she said. "I believe it's unfair that the rest of the family be punished for the sin of one person."

Her father looked surprised at this. "We are speaking of Philip's *mother*. She has shamed her family, and they now bear that shame."

"The shame is dire, yet, do you not think Philip innocent of his mother's choices?" Julia asked. "He did not make those choices for himself."

Her father's brows drew together. "Philip was raised by this woman, and surely she influenced him greatly."

It was hard to argue with that. But Julia took a deep breath, thinking of all she'd learned from Anna and Elisabeth and their stories. "Even if Philip was influenced by his mother, his actions in the village and his hard work have shown him to be a man of integrity and devotion." She glanced at Anna, who was holding back a proud smile. That gave Julia even more courage. "Father, if Philip's mother hadn't abandoned her family, would there be any other objection to him?"

Her father rubbed his face. This gave Julia hope because it meant he might be thinking about her words.

"It is more complicated than that, I'm afraid," he finally said. "There would be no other objection to Philip—although the objection is a serious one—but news about the village is that Bartholomew has requested your hand."

Julia gasped. "I thought no one knew about that."

"I thought so too," her father said. "But your mother has heard gossip from more than one person at the village well. Others know about it, and now they are speculating as to why you are really here with your aunt. They think you have been unfaithful."

It was Julia's turn to rub her face. She wasn't even officially betrothed to Bartholomew, but the label of unfaithful woman would leave a black mark on her for the rest of her life.

"The only way to remedy the idle talk is to accept Bartholomew's hand," her father said. "It will show he has not turned you out and that you are an acceptable bride."

Julia didn't know how to answer. This news was even worse than she had expected. "What does . . . Bartholomew say?"

"He said that if you agree, he wants to still marry you," her father said.

The tension in the room was high as Julia felt her father's expectations, and her mother's from afar. If Julia would agree to this one thing, her family would keep their good standing in the community.

Yet she had done nothing wrong. She'd come to Anna's because her parents had brought her here. It wasn't reasonable to expect her to control gossip in the village. Even if she did agree to marry Bartholomew, would there be gossip about something else?

Anna stayed quiet, letting the discussion stay between Julia and her father. For a moment, Julia wished her aunt would intervene somehow, but what could Anna do?

"You need to know that this has brought your mother great distress," her father continued. "She has been confined to her bedchamber these past two days."

This only made Julia feel worse. "Is Mother ill?"

"Her heart is ill," her father said. "She cannot bear gossip about her daughter."

Julia exhaled. Her mother was a quiet but industrious woman. For her to take to her bed was grave indeed. "I will come home," she said at last. "I will tend to mother, and then we can discuss how to fix what has happened." She expected her father to look joyful, but he gave only a solemn nod.

"We will travel as soon as you can gather your things so as not to delay another day," her father said. He picked up a honey cake Anna had provided, then took a bite as if there were to be no more discussion.

But Julia felt her eyes sting with tears. She looked at Anna, their hostess, and said, "May I be excused?"

"Of course," Anna said.

Julia hurried into her bedchamber just as the tears fell onto her cheeks. She'd miss all of it. Mary's arrival at the temple. Philip visiting with Simeon. Spending her days in Anna's company as they sewed and served. She wiped at her tears and started to gather her things. She would return home to comfort her mother. Then she would make her decision, although things looked bleak enough that she already knew what it would be.

She stood in the middle of the bedchamber for a moment, not moving, while the voices of her father and aunt filtered through the house, soft and indistinguishable. She had only one thing in her power left to do. She crossed to her sleeping mat and knelt. Then she clasped her hands together and raised her face to the heavens.

"O Lord, O God . . ." she began. She had never prayed so earnestly in her life. She prayed for her mother's health. She prayed for Simeon to live to see the Messiah. She prayed for Anna's good health and that she might meet Mary and the child Messiah. She prayed for her father to feel comforted. She prayed for Philip and his brother Seth's success. She prayed for Bartholomew, that whatever the outcome of their relationship might be, it would be blessed by the Lord. She prayed for Elisabeth, her husband, and their son John, that Elisabeth and Zacharias might live a good number of years, so they could see their babe grow into adulthood.

When she finished her prayer, she realized she'd prayed for everyone but herself. Yes, she had needs and desires, but she found she was more concerned with everyone else's needs.

More tears had fallen during her prayer, and she wiped them away with the edge of her sleeve. It took only a few more moments to finish gathering her things into the single satchel she'd brought with her. She'd leave Anna with what she'd bought at the market over the past weeks.

When she walked back into the gathering room, her aunt was clearing the refreshments and her father stood waiting.

"Are you ready, daughter?" he asked.

"Yes, I have everything." She tried to keep her trembling voice calm. She didn't want to break down in front of her father and Anna. She could be strong. Anna had taught her that much.

Julia embraced Anna, holding back the tears, and said good-bye to the woman who had become her best friend.

CHAPTER
TWENTY-THREE

THE HOUSE WAS ABSOLUTELY SILENT when Julia entered. Not even an oil lamp had been lit, though it was well past dark. The knot that had been in her stomach since she first saw her father's cart now grew larger. She hurried into the house, smelling the mustiness that hadn't been there before. Had her mother stopped cleaning as well?

Behind her, she heard her father enter, then scrabble around to light a lamp. So by the time Julia reached her mother's bedchamber, a faint glow lit the way. Julia pushed back the curtain and saw a form huddled on the platform bed. She remembered the day her father had completed building it and how proud he was to show it off to their neighbors.

Julia had helped gather the straw to stuff the mattress, and her mother now kept a couple of trunks beneath the bed, giving them more space to move around in their bedchamber.

"Mother?" Julia said in a quiet voice in case her mother was sleeping. She walked closer, her eyes adjusting to the darkness. "Eunice? Mother?"

Her mother stirred and blinked her eyes open. "Julia."

"It's me," Julia said. "I've returned from Jerusalem."

Her mother didn't say anything for a moment, but Julia could feel her gaze.

"Are you hungry?" Julia asked.

"No," her mother said in her faint voice.

Her father spoke from the doorway. "She always says that."

Julia turned to see her father coming into the room. He carried a platter with some bread and a peeled melon on it. He handed it to Julia. "See if you can encourage her to eat." His voice was gruff, but Julia heard the anguish in it.

When her father left the room, she set the platter on the bed beside her mother. "When is the last time you ate?"

Her mother gave a slight shrug. Finally, she said, "I don't remember."

Julia wasn't used to being her mother's caretaker, but she reached over and rubbed her arm. "Come, let's sit up, and I'll help you eat."

"I'm not a child," her mother said.

"Of course you're not," Julia said as if she were speaking to a child. "We need some light in here."

"I don't want any light."

Julia fought a smile. Her mother sounded exactly like a petulant child. Julia got her to eat a few bites of the roll, although she wouldn't touch the melon. Then Julia fetched an oil lamp and lit it despite her mother's protests.

"There," Julia said when the room was filled with a faint glow. "Now I can brush your hair."

Her mother put her hand to her head. "What's wrong with my hair?"

"Nothing," Julia said, biting back another smile. She didn't know why she felt so content to be here with her mother, away from Anna and Philip and the events at the temple. She supposed it was because she knew her first priority should be to put others' needs before her own. And her mother and father were in need.

She set the platter on a low table in the corner of the room, then fetched the hairbrush her mother had used on her when she was a little girl. She climbed onto the bed and settled next to her mother. "Sit up, and I'll brush," she said in an authoritative voice. Surprisingly, her mother didn't protest, but instead, obeyed.

Julia began to brush through the tangles. Her mother was a slight woman and usually wore her hair in a tight bun. To have the dark hair loose made Julia realize that it had been years since she'd seen her mother with her hair down. She brushed and brushed, and her mother began to relax. From time to time, Julia heard her father in the other room, shuffling around. She was certain he was listening for them but didn't want to interrupt.

Julia continued to brush, even though her mother's hair was smooth by now.

"How is Anna?" her mother finally asked.

"She is very well," Julia said. "She is a gracious hostess, and I feel blessed that I was able to stay with her." In truth, Julia still wanted to be in Jerusalem. But helping her mother was more important.

"It sounds as if Anna has made her life a success despite being a widow with no children," her mother said.

Julia bristled at the comment, but she didn't respond. She was just grateful her mother was talking now.

"The village gossips say Anna has been disobedient for not taking another husband and raising children to the Lord," her mother said. "Yet, I think dedicating one's life to service as Anna has done is an equally noble way to live. Perhaps . . . perhaps not every woman has to follow the same path."

This comment surprised Julia. She agreed with it but hadn't expected her mother to as well. All her life, Julia's parents had been worried about what a neighbor might think about this and that.

"Tell me what her life is like," her mother said.

So Julia began to talk about Anna—about her home, her garden, her neighbors, her sewing. And then she told her mother about the service Anna did in the temple in caring for the mantles the women wore in the Court of Women. She told her mother about the priests' robes that Anna had embroidered.

Her mother nodded as Julia brushed. Then Julia found herself telling her mother about Anna's marriage to Josiah—about how he'd been a widower and hadn't wanted to remarry. About how the village had had to defend itself time after time. And finally, how Michael had become seriously injured in the same battle that had killed Josiah.

"Anna made such a promise to the Lord?" her mother said incredulously. "Surely, she made it out of desperation, not intending to keep it."

"She intended to keep it," Julia said. "And it seems that she did. From the time her brother healed, Anna started working in the temple, devoting the rest of her days to service when other women with families weren't able to."

Her mother turned her head to look at Julia, and she saw the tears in her eyes.

"Does she regret her promise?" her mother asked.

"No," Julia said with confidence. "She is happy, content. She has many friends and good relationships. She lives a peaceful existence, knowing she is serving her Lord."

Her mother took the brush out of Julia's hand. "Turn around."

Julia did so, and her mother unplaited Julia's hair and then began to brush.

"I have missed you," her mother said.

That comment reached deep into Julia's heart. She'd missed her mother as well.

"I'm glad you've returned home," her mother continued. "Although I know that once you marry, you'll go live with your husband's family. So I should get used to you being absent."

It was how life worked, Julia knew. The sons would bring their wives home. The daughters would leave their family and go live with their in-laws. Julia turned to look at her mother. "Whatever happens, I won't be far away." She didn't have the heart to tell her mother that she might not marry at all. Or that if she married Philip, they might have to move to another village to escape the prejudices.

"I have been selfish," her mother said, blinking rapidly.

Julia realized her mother was on the verge of tears. "You haven't been selfish." She took the brush and set it down, then wrapped an arm around her mother and gave her a hug.

"First, I failed at giving your father a son." Her mother wiped the tears spilling onto her cheeks. "Then I had only one daughter, so all burdens are now upon you."

Julia heard her father shuffling around in the next room, and she wondered if he could hear what her mother was saying or if it was something she'd confided to him before.

"I am blessed to be your daughter," Julia said, trying to smile when her mother's words gave her sorrow.

Her mother's tears seemed to start anew. "I should not be standing in the way of your happiness, your life. My life is with your father, and we had a child together. I am well taken care of. We have food, a nice home, good health. We have peace and love. I cannot ask for more."

Julia nodded. She agreed but didn't understand what her mother's intentions were.

"I have made a mistake," her mother said. "At least I thought it was a mistake until you came into my bedchamber tonight."

"What is it?" Julia asked, more confused than ever.

"I have let my fears affect my love for you and my desire for you to be happy." Her mother picked up the brush again and turned it over in her hands as if she were examining it. "I got into an argument with our neighbor Ruth the other day. It's why I have secluded myself. I haven't even told your father the entirety." Her mother spoke in a soft voice, but Julia was certain her father could hear their conversation if he tried.

When her mother seemed to fall silent, lost in thought, Julia asked, "What happened with Ruth?"

"I took her a few of our melons because we had an abundance," she said slowly. "She had been ill, and I thought she might appreciate a small gift. Ruth did appreciate it, but then she asked after you. I don't know why I felt defensive because she was just being kind." She paused. "At least that's what I thought at first. She seemed to question why we had sent you away so suddenly and implied that perhaps you were with child."

Shock coursed through Julia even though her father had told her something similar. Ruth's comment had taken it much, much further. If their neighbor had gone so far as to suggest such a thing to Julia's own mother, then what did the other villagers think?

Her mother took a deep breath. "I told Ruth you are a virtuous woman and that you were visiting a relative. This was all true. Then I said any man would be lucky to have you for a wife and that she should stop spreading lies."

Julia stared at her mother. "You were so bold?"

Her mother nodded. "I couldn't stop there. Once I started defending you, I couldn't hold back any of my opinions. I told Ruth it was wicked to lie and anyone who spoke against my daughter was a liar. I even said that at least Philip's mother was honest—she didn't believe in our God, so she left. She was being more honest than the village gossips."

Julia's mouth fell open. She might have thought these things, but to actually say them to another person was a different matter.

"Ruth was stunned, as you can imagine," her mother said. "It was too late to take back what I'd said, so I don't really blame Ruth when she told me she'd also heard another rumor—that you were carrying Philip's baby."

All the warmth in Julia's body seemed to flee, then the anger set in.

Her mother grasped her hand. "I was so upset. I told Ruth I would be proud to call Philip a son-in-law, but I wouldn't stand for her defaming my daughter's reputation. I took back the basket of melons I had given her."

Julia covered her mouth with her hand, unsure whether to laugh or cry.

Her mother wrapped her arms about Julia and said, "I am sure no one in the village will speak to me now, and I can only imagine what they are saying. Ruth will have them all turned against me—and you—and it's all my fault."

Julia hugged her mother back. "I don't even know what to say."

"I know what to say," her father's voice came from the doorway.

Julia turned to look at her father, and her mother pulled away, her eyes wide.

"I am sorry," her mother whispered, and Julia wasn't sure who she was speaking to.

"You did right by defending our daughter." Her father walked into the room and sat on the edge of the bed. "Ruth has always had a cruel tongue. And until it was directed at our family, we have always looked the other way. No longer."

Julia exchanged glances with her mother.

"Tomorrow, I will speak with the village elders and explain to them what has gone on."

"I don't want to make things worse," her mother said, her tone worried.

Her father took her hand. "My family has lived here for generations, and I won't let a few bad seeds destroy our good name."

"But then what will happen?" her mother asked. "Ruth might apologize, but it won't be sincere. And our daughter will take the brunt of my argument."

Julia had never heard her mother counter her father's opinion. She didn't know if she should leave so they could talk alone. She made a move to climb off the bed, but her mother grasped her hand.

"Silas," her mother said. "If Julia and Philip want to marry, I would like to give them permission, granted that you agree. Don't turn down Philip on *my* account. I do not hold friendships with most of the women in the village anymore, and I do not care what they might say about me. They already think I am cursed because I bore no sons. One more curse in their eyes will make no difference to me."

Julia had never considered that the reason her mother was such a quiet woman and kept mostly to herself was because the other women in the village weren't friendly toward her. The ways of God were mysterious, and while one woman might have a brood of sons and another woman was made barren, the women were left to live with the consequences of either an abundance or lack of blessings.

Her father hadn't said anything for a few moments, but when he did speak, Julia felt warmth spread through her at his words. "I will keep my mind open, and I will travel to Jerusalem and have a conversation with Philip." His gaze slid to Julia's. "I am not making any promises. Having learned about the exchange between your mother and our neighbor Ruth has opened my eyes to how much we have been making family decisions based on what other people may or may not think of us. We need to make our decisions according to what the Lord would have us do."

At that moment, Julia knew that God had heard her prayers and her pleading. Whatever the outcome and whatever decision her father made, Julia knew she could reconcile herself to it. Because her father had heard her, her mother had heard her, and God had heard her. Now she just had to keep having faith.

CHAPTER
TWENTY-FOUR

Julia's father took action the very next day. He set off toward Jerusalem just as dawn broke over the eastern hills. Julia and her mother, who had finally roused herself, stood in the front courtyard and watched him leave. The village was quiet in the early morning, and for a few moments, Julia had a hard time holding any malice toward the villagers.

She turned to look at her mother. The woman had dark circles under her eyes, but her eyes themselves were bright. She smiled and linked arms with Julia. "Ready to begin a new day?"

Her cheerfulness warmed Julia, and she smiled back. "I'm ready. Do we need to go to the market? I didn't see many food-stuffs in the cooking room."

Her mother hesitated, then said, "We will go to the market together, and we will hold our heads high. We have nothing to be ashamed of."

This was a new mother, and Julia loved her.

The two women spent time weeding the garden in the cool morning air, and then Julia swept out the house, noticing that her mother's housekeeping had, indeed, been neglected. After their morning meal, they set off toward the small village market.

Julia felt trepidation as they neared Ruth's house. The woman wasn't in her yard or garden, so they passed by without incident. When they reached the market, it was as if a hush fell over the whole place.

Julia ignored the stares and strode toward Thomas, who was selling grain. He nodded as they approached, although his gaze was more wary than friendly. Her mother purchased a sack of barley, and Julia carried the sack as they made their way to one of the farmers' carts. They picked out a few cucumbers, something that her mother had run out of from her own garden.

No one at the market spoke to them, although Julia saw several women who she thought would normally greet her and her mother. And she didn't want to force them to speak to her. It seemed Ruth had done a thorough job of spreading rumors.

Julia swallowed down the lump that had formed in her throat. She didn't feel sorry for herself; she felt sorry for her mother. Julia didn't see any of her own friends. Two of them were newly married and were probably home tending to their houses. And a third friend was with child and should be delivering soon.

"Do you want to look at anything else?" her mother said in a bright voice.

Julia knew she was just being polite, that her mother didn't really want to stay. "Let's return home and begin preparations for our meal. Hopefully, Father will return by then."

"With good news," her mother said.

How Julia wished that would be the case. They left the market, carrying their purchases, and Julia felt a weight lift. They were no longer surrounded by silent and sullen people. The sharpness of their stares and the sense of what they must be thinking began to fade, and Julia's step was light by the time they reached home. As she helped her mother prepare the meal, Julia focused on her blessings.

Her health and that of her parents. Her experiences with Anna and all that she'd learned. And this opportunity to spend time with her mother doing simple but meaningful tasks. Her mother took a nap about halfway through the afternoon, and Julia was glad she did. She was worried about her mother's thinness and the dark circles beneath her eyes.

When the sun was setting and casting long shadows throughout the house, Julia lit the oil lamps so that when her mother came out of her bedchamber, the house looked warm and cheery. Julia had already set the table, and the barley and pepper stew was steaming in its kettle.

"Any sign of Father yet?" her mother asked.

"Not yet." Julia had been listening to every sound that might resemble someone opening the courtyard gate or footsteps coming across the paving stones.

"Thank you for all of this; it looks wonderful." Her mother stepped forward and embraced Julia.

Julia was surprised. Her help wasn't any different from what she'd done in the past, but it seemed her mother was internalizing everything more than usual. Julia knew it was due to the cruelty of the other villagers, specifically Ruth.

It was as she released her mother that she heard the sound of the gate. Both women rushed to the front door, and Julia's mother opened it.

"Silas," she called out.

Julia studied her father, the set of his shoulders, the manner of his walk, and the expression on his face. He looked tired, nothing more. She couldn't detect what manner of day he'd had, if he'd met with Philip in Jerusalem, or how their conversation had gone.

"Come in," her mother said, holding the door wide.

Her father stepped inside and, in a rare display of affection, stooped and kissed his wife and then Julia on the cheek.

Julia felt her heart leap with hope. Did this mean his news would be what she wanted to hear? Her breathing seemed shallow as she shut the door behind her father. He said something about having to wash before their meal.

Julia hurried into the cooking room and ladled up the stew. When her father returned, they all sat around the table that was used informally when they didn't have guests. Her father blessed the food, and Julia had to force herself to eat despite the nervous knotting of her stomach. She knew she couldn't press him for an answer; she had to wait until he was ready to share his news.

The sun had completely set by the time her father was finished with his meal, and the glow of the oil lamps made the room feel even cozier. Julia exchanged glances with her mother as they cleared away the bowls and brought out a bowl of dates drizzled with honey. Her mother's eyes were alert, her face tense. She was as nervous as Julia, whose fate was about to be announced.

"Thank you for the meal," her father said as Julia and her mother returned to the table. "The journey back home was long and arduous. I helped a man who had lost his way, and that became an unexpected detour."

Julia nodded, while inside, she was wishing he would tell them how the errand of his journey had gone.

"Did you see Philip?" her mother asked.

Julia hid a smile at her mother's outburst. It seemed her mother had become quite vocal during Julia's month-long absence at her aunt's home.

When her father's mouth twitched with the slightest smile, Julia didn't know if she could stand the wait any longer.

"I did see Philip," her father said, stealing a glance at Julia, then refocusing back on her mother. "I asked him many questions." He paused and picked up a date.

Was her father trying to torture her?

He chewed and swallowed. "I asked him about his mother and what sort of life he led after she left," her father continued.

Shock rippled through Julia. She'd never dare ask something so personal. She was almost afraid of what Philip had answered.

"Philip assured me that he had forgiven his mother of her actions, and he made sure to find ways to help his father and brother in her absence." Her father picked up another date but didn't eat it yet. "As you know, after his father died, Philip went into the blacksmithing business with his brother."

Julia exhaled. She was grateful to hear so many details of their conversation, but she still couldn't read her father's expression concerning the outcome.

"From all accounts in the village, he has been honest and hardworking." He looked directly at Julia. "I asked Philip how he planned to provide for a wife."

Julia couldn't breathe now; she could barely think. Did this mean . . . ?

Her mother grasped her hand and squeezed. Julia squeezed back.

"Philip told me his brother is building a house, and that by next season, Philip will have his parents' home to himself," her father said. "I told him that sounded like a fine plan."

Julia waited.

And then it came.

"Philip asked for your hand in marriage, Julia," he said. "And I gave him my blessing."

Julia clapped a hand over her mouth as she let out a shriek. Her mother laughed and pulled her into her arms. And then the two were hugging and crying at the same time. When Julia could finally think, she rose from her chair and hurried to her father's side. She kissed him and then threw her arms about his neck.

He patted her arm and chuckled. But Julia saw the tears in his eyes too.

"I can't believe it, Father," she said.

Her mother rose to her feet too and embraced her husband. "When is the betrothal to take place?"

"Ah," her father said as if it were the farthest thing from his mind. "I have perhaps been hasty in this regard."

Both women stared at him.

"Tomorrow, Philip will arrive," her father said. "We will do the betrothal ceremony here with our local elder. Then we will travel to Jerusalem and stay with Anna for a few days."

"Anna?" her mother said.

But Julia's mind was still reeling with the fact that Philip would be here *tomorrow* and they'd become betrothed—making promises to each other as if they were already married.

"Philip told me of a series of miracles that have happened over the past months," he said, his eyes back on Julia. "I took the time to visit with Anna as well. She claims that a woman named Mary will be visiting the temple in a few days for her purification sacrifice. This Mary is believed to have given birth to the Messiah."

Julia's mother gasped. "You speak blasphemy."

Her father put a hand over his heart. "On my life, I have listened to Anna's account, and I believe in what she says."

Julia's pulse pounded in her ears. Philip had trusted her father enough to tell him. This meant that Philip believed her and Anna as well.

Her mother looked at Julia. "What are these stories that Anna has told your father?"

Julia swallowed, then began to relay their visit to Elisabeth and how they'd met the infant John. Her mother asked questions as Julia spoke, but mostly, she listened. Her father asked a few questions as well.

When Julia finished, her mother had tears in her eyes.

"Remarkable," she kept saying over and over.

Remarkable indeed.

Julia did not sleep that night, *could* not sleep. It wasn't until the first rays of dawn split the sky that Julia fell into a deep sleep, one that lasted less than an hour. When she opened her eyes, she could hear her mother and father speaking in low tones in their bedchamber. She arose and combed through her hair, then plaited it.

She was exhausted but exhilarated. Her hands shook as she worked on her hair, and then she dressed in the linen tunic her mother had given her the night before.

"Julia?" her mother's voice sounded outside her bedchamber.

"I'm awake," Julia said, and her mother entered the room.

"You look lovely in that." Her mother stepped toward her and kissed her on the cheek. "How are you doing?"

"I'm wondering if I'm in a dream." Julia gave her mother a nervous smile. "I don't quite believe this is all happening."

Her mother fussed over Julia's tunic, then said, "We are so happy for you, and we know that whatever the villagers think, your happiness is more important than their opinions. The elder your father invited to the betrothal ceremony will surely spread the word of the betrothal. Everyone will know soon enough."

Julia nodded. "It's just as well. I can live with whatever the cost will be in marrying Philip."

Her mother squeezed her hand, then stepped back just as her father greeted someone at the front door. Philip's deep voice sounded above her father's.

"Philip's here." Julia took a deep breath. Perhaps someday she'd be able to comprehend all of the miracles in her own life.

"I will tell him you're almost ready," her mother said with a smile, then hurried from the room.

Julia looked into the small brass mirror in her room, checking her hair and her face. She was grateful to see that she didn't have dark circles under her eyes from her lack of sleep. Another miracle.

When she joined her family in the gathering room, she couldn't take her eyes off Philip. He wore an indigo-colored robe over a lighter tunic, and he'd combed his hair back and tied it with a leather tie. He looked as if he'd washed recently, which told her he'd stopped at his house on his way. He smiled at her as she met his brown-eyed gaze, and her heart rate increased its galloping pace.

Her blush was quick to rise, and she pulled her gaze away and greeted the elder who had come to be a witness to the ceremony. Uriah was a thin man, perhaps a decade older than her father, his hair streaked with gray. Julia was grateful for his kind eyes and accepting manner. Perhaps the gossip hadn't reached him, or he didn't give credence to such talk.

"Shall we begin?" her father said.

Julia nodded, feeling another blush rise. She stepped forward to the center of the room, and Philip joined her there. She could smell his clean scent mixed with a fresh spice of some sort.

The elder pronounced both of their full names and lineage, then gave a short blessing. "You may join hands now," he continued.

Julia placed her hand in Philip's. The solid and sure warmth of his hand made her feel like she'd stepped into a warm spring meadow, surrounded by an overload of senses.

"In the eyes of God, you are now betrothed. Upon the day of your marriage, you will begin a new family and raise your children to honor God," the elder said as part of his final blessing. He nodded to Philip, who then removed his outer robe and placed it over Julia's shoulders, symbolizing the protection he would give her and the obedience she would give him.

Julia met Philip's eyes, and his smile made her feel like she was floating. She wished they could be alone together and talk privately. She wanted to hear about his perspective of the conversation he'd had with her father. She wanted to tell him about what her mother had gone through and how they could help her in the future. But most of all, she wanted to be his wife and begin their lives together.

Her mother brought out wine and honey cakes for everyone. She must have made the cakes earlier, when Julia had been sleeping. The elder stayed for refreshments, then Julia's father sent him home with a basket of olives from the grove.

Julia still didn't have any privacy with Philip. She and her parents prepared for their trip while Philip helped load their cart and feed their donkey. She and her mother rode in the cart with their belongings and the few baskets of olives her father would trade for a lamb at the main Jerusalem market during their sojourn.

Her father and Philip walked, and Julia and Philip exchanged plenty of glances and smiles. She still wore his robe, and she wondered if she'd ever take it off. She didn't even mind the heat from the persistent sun as they traveled.

By the time they reached Anna's home, everyone was ready for a rest. Anna must have returned from the temple early because she was home to greet them. She immediately offered cool water from the well, and Julia helped her prepare fruit for everyone.

Her mother still refused to eat any melon, instead choosing to eat a couple of figs and a piece of day-old flatbread.

While everyone relaxed on the cushions in the gathering room, Julia insisted on helping Anna begin the meal preparations. She sat at the table with Anna as they seeded pomegranates.

"You are betrothed, I see," Anna said quietly so as not to let her voice carry into the other room.

Julia grinned. "Since this morning."

"It has all happened so fast," Anna said. "At least one would think so. God's ways can be swift."

"I have been praying so much that I think I finally wore God down," Julia said.

Anna chuckled. "I have been praying for you as well. Perhaps God wanted to move on to other concerns, so He found a way to quiet us."

They shared another smile. In truth, Julia was still having a hard time believing she was not living in the middle of a wonderful dream. "Have you seen Elisabeth or heard any news about Mary?"

"Nothing yet," Anna said, her eyes bright. "I have been counting the days. This morning, the purification sacrifices were done by other women but not Mary. I did see Simeon at the temple, and we spoke for a few moments."

"We will all go to the temple tomorrow with you," Julia said. "My father wants to do a peace offering."

Anna smiled. "I hope it will be a wonderful day, then. Although every day at the temple is wonderful, of course."

Julia's heart was full, and she marveled that she was surrounded by so many blessings. She didn't know what her future would be as Philip's wife. Would they have children? Would she be barren like Anna? Would she and Philip live to an old age? Would the village accept their marriage? So many unknowns, yet she was beginning to learn that if she put her trust in the Lord, her concerns and worries were eased.

They served and ate supper in the back courtyard as the sun set. Anna told everyone that as a child, it was a tradition with her father and brother. As they ate and talked, the shadows grew long and the evening cooled, but everyone was reluctant to go inside.

Julia and the other women cleared the platters of food and brought out a round of wine for everyone. When the night grew deep and the oil lamps dimmed, Julia's parents excused themselves, followed by Anna.

Philip looked across the table at Julia, his eyes nearly black in the dim light. "I never thought we'd be alone."

Julia smiled, tired as she was. "I didn't either." She felt suddenly shy, sitting here alone with him. Even though there was a table between them, her skin was warming up. "I couldn't believe the news my father brought me last night. I thought for sure he would reject my suggestion. But when he told me he was going to come to Jerusalem to meet with you, I finally allowed myself to hope."

Philip's gaze held hers, and she marveled that she was betrothed to this man. He rose and snuffed out the oil lamps, so they were left in the natural darkness of the night. The moon and the stars made the courtyard seem ethereal somehow. Philip walked around the table, then he held his hand out.

She hesitated for a moment but only because she was starting to blush again. She set her hand in his, and he drew her up beside him. He didn't move away immediately but looked down at her.

"You look tired," he said. "Beautiful, but tired."

"I am tired, but I'm happy too." She wanted to lean into him, to breathe him in, to wrap her arms around him. But she remained still.

"Come into the house so you can rest," he said, tugging on her hand and guiding her to the back door. There, they stood beneath the overhanging roof, and Julia felt cocooned in the dark with him.

It was warm next to him, and when he said, "You look good wearing my robe," she felt her face heat up even more.

Thankfully, the darkness concealed her blushing.

Philip rested a hand on her shoulder, and before she could gather her thoughts of how his touch was making her feel, his hand slid behind her neck and he leaned down and gently kissed her. His mouth was warm, his lips soft, his scent sweet like the wine they'd drunk after their meal.

Julia placed a hand on his chest, feeling the thumping of his heart, and lifted up on her toes to kiss him back.

All too soon, he drew away, capturing her hand in his. He brought her hand to his lips and pressed another kiss to her palm.

"I'll see you in the morning," Philip said, releasing her and opening the door.

She walked in ahead of him. An oil lamp was burning in the cooking room, casting shadows about the corridor leading to the bedchambers. She'd be sharing a room with her parents and sleeping on a mat. Philip would be sleeping in the gathering room on the cushions.

With Philip leaning against the wall, watching her, she walked down the corridor, then glanced back at him before slipping into the bedchamber. Philip smiled, and in that smile, she saw a bright future.

CHAPTER TWENTY-FIVE

As DAWN LIGHTENED THE SKY, Anna wasted no time in rising and preparing the morning meal for her guests. She would be going to the temple early again. She'd gone to the temple every morning for the past week, hoping to be there when Mary and Joseph came.

"You're awake," Julia said, walking into the cooking room.

Anna stopped stirring the barley cereal she was warming over the coals. Julia looked radiant, and Anna was so pleased that her niece was happily betrothed. "Good morning."

"Can I help?" Julia asked.

"You can cut up some figs to mix them in with this cereal." She pointed to the basket of figs.

"Are you not eating?" Julia asked, noting the number of bowls set on the table.

Anna turned to face her niece. "I am fasting today. I find that I have much to pray for and be thankful for."

Julia nodded. "I will fast too." She removed one of the bowls.

"What time are you leaving for the temple?" Julia asked.

Anna smiled. "Soon. If your family wants to sleep, I will meet you all there."

"I think we're all coming early," Eunice said, joining them in the cooking room. Sure enough, Silas came in right behind her.

Before Anna could reply, Philip also arrived, looking as if he'd just woken up.

Anna looked at the eager faces watching her. "You are all welcome to come early with me, of course. I can't promise that Mary will be bringing her infant today."

"Of course," Julia's mother said. "We will just be happy to go with you."

Anna's heart swelled. She hadn't been around so much family in years, and to see them all together like this was already its own miracle.

After their morning meal and after Julia had insisted on cleaning up, the group set off toward the temple.

Anna marveled at the three generations of family walking along the road in the early morning sunlight.

The temple grounds were already bustling with activity. Silas found a merchant to trade a lamb for olives, and once they passed through the gate, Anna led the way to the Court of Women. There, they donned the embroidered mantles and began their prayers, while Philip and Silas went into one of the other courts.

Anna had so much to be grateful for, not only in her life but also in becoming a witness to the blessings in others' lives. She didn't know how many more years she had on the earth, but she'd spent the ones she'd had happy and at peace, fulfilling the covenants she'd made with God.

When her prayers were finished, she visited quietly with a few of the women, welcoming them and asking after their families. On the other side of the courtyard, she caught sight of Simeon. He moved slowly due to his age, but his countenance was bright. And he was smiling at something or someone. Then Anna realized he was focused on the line of people waiting to hand over their sacrifices.

Before Anna followed his gaze to a specific couple, she felt her pulse speed up. Could it be?

She scanned the people in line. There was a couple with a baby, but for some reason, Anna didn't think the woman was Mary. Anna kept looking until she saw another couple toward the back of the line. The woman stood next to a tall, bearded man who must be her husband. Her hair was pulled back and plaited down her back, and she wore a pale-blue tunic that looked rumpled but clean. In her arms, she held a small infant.

There was nothing extra to notice about the couple with the babe, but Anna couldn't ignore the countenance of the woman. It reminded her of the innocence and sweetness of a child. The man held a small woven cage that contained two turtledoves—for a purification sacrifice.

Anna couldn't move for a moment, and even when she knew Julia was at her side and had asked a question, she kept staring at the couple. The babe was awake, and both parents kept their gazes on him, not paying attention to anything else going on around them.

Even from a distance, Anna could make out the dark curls and smooth skin of the child. A sacred child. Anna couldn't explain how she knew—but her heart was beating fast, and her eyes were tearing up.

"Anna?" This time it was Eunice's voice. "Are you all right?"

Anna nodded, then shook her head. She gave a little laugh and wiped at her tears. She couldn't really speak or explain. Her throat had tightened, and her heart felt as if it might leap right out of her chest. She had to get closer. She had to see the child for herself.

Still wearing the temple mantle, she walked toward the line of people. She sensed that Julia and her mother were following her, without a word, without a question.

She saw Simeon moving toward the couple as well. Anna smiled through the tears that kept on falling. Simeon's step had quickened, and he walked as if he were a young man. At this pace, he would arrive at the couple before she did.

Then Simeon caught sight of Anna. He smiled at her, and Anna smiled back. They were on opposite sides of the court, but no words needed to be spoken between them since they were both going to the same destination.

The husband looked up as Simeon joined them in line. Anna arrived just as the young mother looked up as well.

"I am Simeon," he said. "Years ago, the Holy Spirit revealed to me that I should not see death before I had seen the Messiah." He lifted his aged and spotted hands. "As you can see, I have waited many years."

The young man stared at Simeon in disbelief.

But the young woman smiled. "I am Mary, and this is my husband, Joseph. Would you like to hold the babe?"

Anna put her hand on her heart as she watched Simeon take the child in his arms. Simeon cradled the child as if he were made of the most precious gold, and because both of his arms were preoccupied, his tears ran freely down his face.

"I can now depart in peace," Simeon said in a trembling voice. "For I have seen salvation. This child will be a light to the Gentiles and the glory of Israel." Simeon looked into Mary's eyes. "This child is the fruit of all the prophesies spoken of Him."

Mary blinked away tears as Simeon handed the child back to her. Then Mary looked at Anna.

Anna stepped forward and tried to smile. She could not speak for a moment, so overcome was she. But Mary held out the child, and Anna placed her hand on the infant's head. The babe's dark eyes seemed very alert for a child so young, and Anna wanted to take Him in her arms like Simeon had, but she didn't trust her strength. Her knees already felt like they might give out.

"Praise the Lord on this day," Anna said, then prophesied, "Our salvation and redemption is here at last. Jerusalem will now be delivered." She smiled tremulously at Mary.

"Thank you for your blessing," Joseph said, looking from Anna to Simeon. "Thank you both. We marvel that you know who our Son is."

"We are grateful to meet you," Mary added.

Anna took a shaky breath. "The honor has been ours." Around them, the people in line had hushed, and others were whispering to each other.

Anna met Silas's gaze. Tears had reddened his eyes as he stood with his arm around his wife and daughter. Philip stood on the other side of Simeon, unable to take his eyes off the child.

"We have all been blessed to be witnesses this day," Anna said.

Simeon wiped his face with the sleeve of his robe. "Go in peace, and may you be protected in all things."

Joseph shook Simeon's hand, then did the same with Silas and Philip.

The line moved forward, and other people spoke to Joseph and Mary.

Anna felt someone grasp her hand, and she looked over at Julia.

The young woman was also crying, yet the smile was broad on her face. "I think I can die happy now, like Simeon," Julia said.

Anna gave a soft laugh. "You have many years ahead of you yet. I hope to meet your children."

Julia leaned forward and embraced Anna. "I hope you will meet them too."

Eunice also stepped forward to embrace Anna. "Thank you for watching over my daughter."

"She will always be welcome," Anna said.

A small crowd had gathered around Joseph and Mary and the Messiah. So Anna led her family out of the Court of Women and through another temple gate, where they could sit in the shade. They found an outcropping of rocks to settle on. As her family discussed what they had seen and heard, Anna let all their words soak into her soul.

Her troubles and concerns would be eased, and she would be made whole—this she knew without a doubt. All those who desired redemption and salvation would be able to find it. The promised Light had arrived. She looked toward the temple and the line of people with their animals to be used as sin, peace, and purification sacrifices.

She closed her eyes as the breeze stirred around her, and the hairs on her arms rose. Her feelings were identical to Simeon's. She could die in peace, knowing that she had lived her life to the fullest, she had served God, she had been a witness to many miracles, she had seen the Messiah . . . and she had shared her love and beliefs with those who had come after her.

ACKNOWLEDGMENTS

THE STORY OF ANNA THE Prophetess has been on my mind for many years. I've often wondered about the character of a woman who faces difficult trials, yet never gives up, and continues to live a life of service. Anna is a wonderful example, and yet, I sense that she had many difficult days. She must have lived on a great amount of faith and truly put her trust in the Lord. I think we can all identify with Anna in many ways.

I'd like to thank those who've helped me on this writing journey, specifically as I prepared this book. First, my parents Kent and Gayle Brown were earlier readers of the manuscript. My father is a New Testament scholar, yet he has always been supportive of my fictional renderings of these deeply layered stories. My mother keeps her friends supplied with copies of my books, and I appreciate the sweet notes I receive in return.

Thanks as well to my father-in-law, Lester Moore, for his unfailing support of my books. He has been a great champion from day one. Thank you to Dave LeFevre, a scholar in his own right who has been generous with his time as I worked on fine-tuning some of the plot points of Anna's experiences.

Many thanks to my publisher Covenant Communications for their enthusiasm and support for this manuscript. I've worked with editor Samantha Millburn for a number of years, and I'm grateful for not only her careful editing but her guidance and friendship. Thanks as well to the rest of the staff, including Stephanie Lacy for marketing, and all her hard work on my behalf.

A final thanks goes to my husband and children for their continuous support!

ABOUT THE AUTHOR

HEATHER B. MOORE IS A *USA Today* best-selling author of more than a dozen historical novels and thrillers written under the pen name H.B. Moore. She writes women's fiction, romance, and inspirational nonfiction under Heather B. Moore. This can all be confusing, so her kids just call her Mom. Heather attended Cairo American College in Egypt and the Anglican School of Jerusalem in Israel and earned a bachelor of science degree from Brigham Young University in Utah. Visit Heather's website here: www. hbmoore.com.